Wil

Che Guevara's Marijuana & Baseball Savings & Loan

Che Guevara's Marijuana & Baseball Savings & Loan

A Novel of the Early Days of the Peace Corps

Jack Shakely

Library of Congress Control Number:		2013910280
ISBN:	Hardcover	978-1-4836-4927-6
	Softcover	978-1-4836-4926-9
	Ebook	978-1-4836-4928-3

This book was printed in the United States of America.

Rev. date: 06/08/2013

To order additional copies of this book, contact:
Xlibris Corporation
1-888-795-4274
www.Xlibris.com
Orders@Xlibris.com
136933

To my friends in
Costa Rica II and El Salvador II

AUTHOR'S NOTE

There is no evidence that Che Guevara was in Nicaragua in 1963. There is no strong evidence of exactly *where* Che Guevara was in large chunks of 1963.

The absence of evidence is not evidence of absence.

CHAPTER

1

The Wall Street Journal called me "Drug Lord of the Peace Corps." Hyperbole, I think, and less than accurate, as usual.

The more restrained New York Times called me "America's 'grass'-roots ambassador." And the Village Voice, playful as ever, dubbed me the raja of ganja and the Peace Corps' prince of pot.

Such sobriquets (87—I'll explain this later) would clearly do damage to my reputation, if I had a shred of one left. But I have drifted beyond dignity.

I am more or less at peace. There's a certain calm that descends upon you when you are no longer driven by ambition. I have passed through that membrane of desire.

It wasn't always so. Once I measured my horizons on epic scales. At one time I had boyhood dreams that I might have a shot at becoming the first Oklahoman to become president—certainly the first mixed-blood Creek ever elected to congress.

I've scaled back my ambitions quite a bit since then. Being accused of almost single-handedly bringing down the Peace Corps hurts, I will admit. And being caught in a marijuana money laundering scheme with Che Guevara, even in the most positive light imaginable, is a career-limiting experience. Not to mention the pound of marijuana they found in my office (thanks, Larry). And then of course there's the money which I readily admit I withdrew, and which was far less than advertised.

Plus there's the undeniable fact that if you want to run for office in the United States, you've got to live there. I am currently in exile; living in an abandoned schoolhouse in an equally-abandoned rubber tree plantation near a farmed-out, petered-out fly-specked village in the Caribbean low country of Nicaragua, not far from Bluefields.

This old rubber plantation used to be crawling with dozens of people—Che Guevara and his rebels intent on overthrowing the hated government of Nicaraguan dictator Luis Somoza. I actually played baseball with El Che and Victor right over there, on the other side of the hen house. The revolution sputtered and died before it ever got going, of course, and those who could still travel high-tailed it to Bolivia. But I figure if the *federales* couldn't find sixty men in these jungles, they sure couldn't find one.

I also kind of like thinking that the best place for a man without a country is in a state without a country. Somoza and his boys couldn't care less if this part of Nicaragua sinks into the sea, and I'm hoping that things will stay that way for a while, maybe quite a while.

I live here with old Casimiro, who's been the caretaker of the plantation since forever. Everybody in the camp thought the old snaggle-tooth was slightly crazy, and he probably is, which is just fine with me. He leaves me alone; I leave him alone. I told him that Che, who Casimiro thinks is a god, will be coming back soon, so be quiet and lie in the weeds. He gave me a conspiratorial wink and five-toothed grin, then went hobbling off.

So I've got some time on my hands until I can find a way to get to Paraguay or some other country that hasn't signed extradition treaties with the United States. I figure that setting down all my adventures on paper will help me clear my thoughts, at least, if not my name. I've got the time and it's not like I have any pressing appointments. The old rubber tree plantation school teacher was kind enough to leave a drawer full of Anaconda brand ball point pens, and it's a cinch Casimiro won't be calling on them. There are also all these little blue examination books. There's a whole box of them. I wonder if anybody else has ever written his memoirs on little blue books. I read somewhere that Tolstoy wrote *War and Peace* in pencil on like a hundred paper tablets, so here we go—*Kiff and Peace; Peace and Doobies.*

Just a note before I start laying out the whole story—some of the stuff I'm going to write about took place in English and some in Spanish, and I may have to use a little Spanish from time to time. But I'll try not to be cute about it. I'll stick to English as much as possible. I don't know about you, but I get a little tired of those books that take place in Cuba or Mexico or somewhere and everyone is obviously speaking Spanish, but the book's in English except for cute little Spanish words and phrases the author tosses in to remind you where you are. It's usually some gnarly old grandfather who says stuff like "*Si, mi hijita,*" and "*Ay, Diós mio*;" or the author writes *miko* and *pinga* to avoid writing dirty words in English. Not in this book. There probably will be some dirty words, especially if I quote my buddy John McNaughton correctly. But I might as well stick to English—it's as close to the United States as I'm likely to get for a while.

Also I think I'll write about everybody in the past tense, because I don't know anymore who's alive or dead—including me. Sometimes I think maybe I'm dead, living in purgatory or what do they call it—limbo. And while I may be living in the limbo on the other side of the tracks, I'm pretty sure I'm not in hell. Hell doesn't have chickens. Probably.

CHAPTER

2

Chickens in the tropics have, I believe, few natural predators. This is probably lucky for the predators, because the scrawny, feral little raptors that live under my Nicaraguan schoolhouse wouldn't make much of a meal, even for a ferret or a coati.

It was the same in my village in Costa Rica along the riparian jungles near Lake Nicaragua when I was in the Peace Corps. Costa Rican cooks didn't dare serve the ugly, ropey cacklers as a separate dish, but cut them into unrecognizable chunks and disguised them in soups, mounds of rice and peas, even those fat holiday tamales wrapped in banana leaves that made you feel less than happy that Christmas was coming. Yes, that's right—the Peace Corps. I'll get to that.

We had chickens, lot of chickens, when I was growing up in rural Oklahoma. Almost everybody did, and they weren't these feathery losers, either. They were big and plump—White Leghorns, Rhode Island Reds, Brahmas, Plymouth Rocks, Cornish, Wyandottes, fat little banties. I know my chickens. That was my job around the farm when I was just a little guy, feeding them and watering them, bringing in the eggs. Sometimes I even had to chip the ice off the feeders in winter so the birds could drink. Winter seems like a foreign country to me now.

My name is Jack Harjo. Harjo is a Creek word meaning brave or crazy. It was a word most often used in battle, so it comes closer to meaning bold and reckless than nuts. It was a name given in respect and worn proudly. One of the great Creek chiefs from the old days was named Echo Harjo (in the typical Indian way of calling a spade a spade, he was called Echo because he stuttered) and near the turn of the century—"Crazy Snake," Chitto Harjo.

Jack is an English word that can mean a naval flag, the third-highest face card in a deck, money, a six-tipped game piece used with a rubber ball in a game with the same name, an electrical plug, a devise to elevate a car to fix a flat, the act of elevating a car to fix a flat, or nothing (as in you don't know jack). Used in combination with other words it can be a food (jackfruit, Monterey Jack, Cracker Jack, flapjacks, amberjack), stealing, a percussive hammer, a card game, masturbation, a handyman, a mule, a flower and a Halloween pumpkin.

Jack can also be, as in my case, a nickname for John, which sometimes caused me problems in Oklahoma.

"How come your driver's license says John and your check says Jack?" asked the Humpty-Dumpty clerk, her eyes narrowing.

"Cause Jack is a nickname for John," I offered helpfully.

"Nicknames are supposed to be shorter than regular names. That's why we use them. These are the same size."

"I know. I can't really explain that," I said. Then in a moment of inspiration that came from being broke and hungry, I added, "You've heard of John Kennedy and Jack Kennedy, right?"

"Sure."

"Well, they're the same person," I said like a lawyer ending his summation.

"Huh-uh," the clerk said in that friendly sing-song tone that means not only do I know you're wrong, but I think you're trying to pull my leg. "One of them's the daddy."

My daddy was John Harjo, semi-retired farmer and extremely lucky holder of mineral rights on eighty acres of land in the Turner Basin near Ardmore. This didn't make us Cadillac-rich, but those two little grasshopper oil wells in the south forty kept us in new Buicks and nice clothes, and Mother in cigarettes. The money came in four times a year, regular as rain water, as they say.

Daddy was enough of an Indian that he got on the roles, which made him an official Indian. I'm only an eighth, which means I'm Indian to white people, and white to Creeks. Sort of the story of my life, I guess. Square peg.

My mother was a chain smoker, a gifted writer and anarchist. Lung cancer got her when I was still a senior in high school. My mother's name was Elizabeth Langhorne Harjo, or so I thought, and she was one sharp cookie. She was a graduate of the University of Missouri's school of journalism and wrote a twice-weekly column for the local newspaper, *The Ardmorite*. Her column was called "Out of Left Field by Elizabeth Langhorne Harjo."

One day when I was in the sixth grade, I came running home from school where we'd been reading "Tom Sawyer." "Mother," I shouted, "Mark Twain's real name was Samuel Langhorne Clemons. Are we *those* Langhornes? Are we related to Mark Twain?"

Mother laughed softly. "No, child. I just use that name as an innocent homage to the great man. I had a professor who said most great writers have three names, and I thought Harjo needed a little fluffing out. If you promise to keep a secret, I'll tell you my real maiden name."

I nodded my head uncertainly.

"Welcher. Can you imagine going through life with that hanging around your neck? 'So your daddy's a welcher?' 'You wouldn't welch on us, would you, Welcher?' I think reason number four or five that I married your daddy was to trade in my last name."

"What was reason number one?"

"Your daddy was, and is, the best-looking man I ever did see. You got his looks, Jack. Now it's my job to get your brain to the same high level, and Tom Sawyer's a real fine place to start. Bring your book here in the kitchen. You can read while I type."

Mother was tickled by the Out of Left Field title of her column, which was actually Daddy's idea. "Half the people who start reading it will think it's about sports," she said with that smoker's laugh that sounded a bit like a coughing sea lion. "By the time they get to paragraph three, I can sink my Let's Hear It for the Little Man hooks into them. If I haven't got 'em by then I don't want 'em anyway, they're too dumb."

Her column was popular unless you were a governor, state senator or county commissioner. "Left field, hell," Governor Murray yelled one day at a rally over at Madill. "She's a commie pinko." Daddy said that was nonsense; she was an equal opportunity bomb-thrower.

Both Daddy and I were in awe of my mother, adored her, but she could be a little stand-offish. When he came to visit the newspaper one day, Governor Murray told her that Elizabeth Langhorne Harjo sounded mighty formal. "What do your friends call you?" he boomed with that laugh-that's-not-a-laugh.

"Elizabeth Langhorne Harjo," she answered demurely. "But you can keep calling me Commie Pinko. I'm starting to like it."

Mother could also be razor-blade funny, both in her columns and in person. One of her finest moments came when she was asked to participate on a panel with Congressman Arthur Wickerman at an Arrows to Atoms Semicentennial Celebration debate at Oklahoma City University in 1957 (by the way, although Oklahomans have a reputation for being unlettered, every single one of us knows what semicentennial means, thanks to us becoming a state in 1907 and our not being able to wait a hundred years to celebrate).

The debate was about the "one man—one vote" concept that was working its way to the US Supreme Court. Congressman Wickerman, who had already erected an "Impeach Earl Warren" sign in his front yard, despised the idea. Wickerman was a short, fleshy man who made you think he had a cigar in his mouth, even when he didn't. He, like Governor Murray, hated communists and found them in every corner of America, especially universities and newspapers, waiting to pounce on unsuspecting Okies while we slept.

Congressman Wickerman never met an oilman or rancher he didn't like and that particular day he was railing about how those Fellow Travelers Eisenhower and Earl Warren were trying to nationalize the oil fields and the cattle industry.

"It's just unbelievable that these communists and socialists can go wading in on election day and outflank and destroy our fine homesteading Oklahoma farmers, ranchers and oilmen," Wickerman said. "Our people are producing things, making things grow, pulling riches out of the ground with their bare hands and a little luck, making life better for all of us. The socialists don't own anything; they just want some of what we got. Do you really think it's right for some socialist on welfare to get the same vote as the man who owns a piece of this fine country, who has a stake in the game? Of course not. Oklahomans are people of the land, and our land has a right to be heard. We're getting shortchanged by those New York socialists, stacked up there like cordwood, voting against the hardworking ranchers and wildcatters who are filling Yankee gas tanks and bellies. Let me say this: if every socialist and his welfare mammy gets one vote, then our hardworking landholders should have two. It's the land that makes us great, and the land should have a voice."

There was a smattering of applause, but the audience hadn't really been expecting such a stem-winder or convoluted logic, and it took us a little by surprise.

"Excuse me, Congressman," Mother interjected. "Are you actually suggesting that dirt should have the vote?"

"Very clever, Miss Langhorne Harjo. I guess newspaper women can twist words just as easily as newspaper men. I'm saying that true Americans who have a stake in this country deserve to determine its destiny. There is no evidence that these socialists and communists even know *how* to run a country. They can't run Russia, and they sure as hell can't run Oklahoma."

"Absence of evidence is not evidence of absence," Mother said.

"Just what the hell does that mean, College Lady?" Wicker-man snorted, unused to being interrupted when he was on a roll.

"Well, let's see if I can explain it, Congressman. Let's just say that even though there is an absence of evidence that you ever learned anything in school; that is not sufficient evidence that your brains are absent." Mother paused and rubbed her chin. "Well, come to think of it, maybe I should choose my examples a little more carefully."

There was a burst of laughter, especially from the predominately student and faculty audience members. They had been waiting for a chance to laugh at that idiot, and Mother gave it to them.

Fuming and actually shaking his fist at my mother, Arthur Wickerman stomped out of the auditorium. He would get the Harjos back, at least one of them.

CHAPTER

3

I hung around the newspaper a lot in high school. If I didn't have baseball practice, I'd head over to the *Ardmorite* after school and get in a good hour of reading and pestering the editorial staff before Daddy came in the pickup to take Mother and me home (like a lot of women who grew up before the war, Mother never learned to drive, and had no real interest in the subject).

Even though the *Ardmorite* was a daily, it only had a handful of employees in what they called the front office. Everybody, including Mother, did double duty and they used a lot of volunteers to write PTA, garden club and local sports stuff. I even got to try my hand from time to time on stories I couldn't screw up: "Leroy Costairs, son of Mr. and Mrs. Clovis Costairs of 821 N. Chickasaw Street, has been promoted to Private First Class. He is currently assigned to headquarters company, Fort Polk, La. where he is a technical specialist in the motor pool. Costairs is a 1956 graduate of Ardmore High School where he lettered in football and track."

I had two favorites at the paper. One was Art Triester, whose gloomy face was as wrinkled as an unmade bed. He was also bald, and his main wrinkles became three ditches that traveled all the way up his head to the back of his neck. Art had the title of advertising manager, although he didn't manage anybody—he was it. He also wrote a weekly column called "Ask Pepper," which was supposed to be written by a woman named Pepper Holiday. Art would make his weekly rounds of the shops that paid ten bucks a week to be featured, and then write a "column" in a breathless, girlie style: "Just in time for Easter, the folks at Marge's Little Shoppe have a new shipment of darling straw hats. There are only a few of the wide-brimmed ones left, so do go down to Marge's today. And be sure to tell them Pepper sent you."

"If you don't mind me saying so, Art, you sort of make Pepper sound like Lucy Ricardo. Is that the way you figure women write?" I asked him one day as we went through the daily task of breaking down the ads and saving the clip art. Over his shoulder I saw my mother roll her eyes and pretend to stick her finger down her throat.

Art feigned concentrating on stripping the tape off a drawing of some oranges he'd used for an IGA grocery store layout. "I know Elizabeth is smirking behind me, but yeah, at least that's how some women write. The advertisers don't complain and people really believe there is a Pepper Holiday. It turns a buck for the paper, too. Besides, she's the only woman columnist," he turned his head toward Mother for effect, "repeat, *only woman columnist,* who gets fan mail every week and not a single death threat."

My other favorite was Old Bob Hogan, the editor. He was probably younger than Art, but he had a lot of mileage on him. He was an alcoholic, I guess, and he had false teeth that rattled in the back of his mouth. This embarrassed him, so when he was on the phone, he'd take his teeth out and drop them in a glass of whiskey he kept on the desk. This was the only whiskey he'd touch until five o'clock, when his left bottom desk drawer would slide open and the bottle of Four Roses would poke its head out.

Mr. Hogan gave himself his nickname. "Come on, Jackson, you can tell Old Bob." He was the best-read man I ever met, with a vocabulary to match. He and I came up with a game where he would give me a new word every day and I was supposed to find the definition and make up a sentence with the word in it for the next day.

"Abstemious, Harjo, abstemious," he'd shout over the constant plinkity-plink of the Linotype machines. "And don't forget to read Lippmann today. He tears ass."

"Yes sir, I will. I sometimes find him *soporific*, but I'll give him another shot."

"Not bad, Jackson. Not your best effort, but not bad," Old Bob shouted again in his clicky-teeth fashion. This was considered high praise from him, and I took it as such.

I did read Walter Lippmann and every other columnist on the AP feed I could get my hands on: Joseph Alsop and his brother Stuart, Arthur Schlesinger when I could find him, even Drew Pierson, who Mother said was nothing more than "Pearl Mesta in pants."

The fact is I read damn near anything and everything—the classics, magazines (it was about this time I started reading the *New Yorker*, but I hid it from my friends the way you hide *Playboy* from your mother), articles, newspapers, boxes of cereal. And maybe because of all the reading and Old Bob's coaching, school was so easy for me I had to start pulling my punches.

In Ardmore High School there were Jocks and there were Brains, but it was risky trying to be both. Tommy Sinclair, who was every bit as smart as me, was the quarterback, so the other guys cut him some slack. But baseball was my sport, and baseball players were supposed to be dumb, or at least ignorant (Old Bob had taught me that there was a difference). Maybe it was the Mickey Mantle effect. The Mick, who was also from Oklahoma, was already playing pro ball when his classmates in Commerce were graduating. He was the Yankee centerfielder when he was only nineteen. When somebody asked him if he ever regretted missing out on college, Mantle said, "Naw, I'm already as smart as I want to be, and smarter than I need to be."

My baseball coach (who was also my history teacher) pulled me aside after practice one day in my junior year. He sat me down on the steps to the dugout, put his arm around me and said, "Jack, now don't take this wrong. I know I'm your teacher and everything. But you've got tons of talent and I think there's a real good chance you can make it to the Bigs. People either play baseball or they go to college. It ain't like football where you can do both. I don't think there's a single college man in professional baseball. Least I can't name one. I say stick to baseball. I might even help a little. I know a scout over in Albuquerque." He looked over his shoulder. "Um, you won't tell you mom we had this little talk, will you?"

Of course I didn't tell her, but it did put a crimp in my thinking. Why be a congressman when you could be a Yankee? I couldn't believe that baseball and learning, two of my three most favorite things in the world, would be lining up on opposite sides of the chalk.

As luck would have it, it was my third love that sorted things out for me.

* * *

The Eagle. To this day, I can't write those words without that gnawing in the pit of my stomach that teenage love engenders. I was desperately in love with the Cushman Eagle, and I knew it would take a full-scale campaign to get one. I spent most of my sophomore and junior years mapping out strategy, polishing arguments, laying traps and leaving hints for my unsuspecting parents.

A Cushman Eagle is a motor scooter. Of course that's like saying Marilyn Monroe is a blond.

Cushman actually used to make two motor scooters—the model 50, or Pacemaker, which everybody hated; and the Eagle, the dream machine, the passport to freedom, the Equalizer.

None of us guys could figure out why they even bothered to make the Pacemaker. It looked exactly like a great big bread box with little wheels and a handlebar. You sat on it like you'd sit on a park bench and it was just about as exciting. We figured it was a fall-back scooter. When your folks said absolutely no to an Eagle, you could hang you head and stare at your shoes and say, "Well, could I at least have a model 50? They're a lot cheaper." That usually didn't work either, but it was one of those last-gasp deals. The only person who had a Pacemaker at Ardmore High was Denise Stufflebean, whose father owned the funeral home and absolutely had no clue. And neither did Denise. Case closed on the 50.

The Cushman Eagle, on the other hand, looked just like a real motorcycle. To be honest, it looked like a real motorcycle that had been left out in the rain and shrunk two sizes. But it had the right kind of seat and a gas tank you straddled and one of those stomp-starters just like the one Marlon Brando had in "The Wild Bunch." It also had plenty of pep for a two-stroke engine. You could get it up to fifty miles an hour no sweat (the speedometer went up to sixty, but the manual warned you about pegging it) and it seemed faster because you were so close to the ground.

But it wasn't speed that I was after. It was prestige; it was adulthood; it was being a man. And maybe, just maybe, it was about getting laid.

Because we lived four miles out of town, I had some logic going for me most of the other guys didn't. Mother not driving didn't hurt either.

I used to lay copies of Argosy and Popular Mechanics magazines around the living room casually open to the Cushman ads. I was shameless. When I turned sixteen, I hit on the idea to ask for a car, so I could drive myself places while Daddy attended to farm chores and such. This didn't fly, as I figured it wouldn't, so I used the Cushman Eagle as *my* fall-back plan. I knew Daddy didn't like tricks, so I came right out and asked for the scooter. To my utter surprise, Daddy didn't say no exactly, even saying how it might teach me to be responsible like when his daddy gave him a horse. But there was a lot of wait-and-see in his voice, so I did.

Finally it was baseball that nudged the needle to my side of the dial. Spring practice would often go on long after school was over, and Mother liked to get home before five so she could fix dinner. Daddy wasn't so hot on picking her up and then going back to town to get me an hour or so later.

"Isn't there anybody you can hitch a ride home with after practice?" Daddy asked one night over dinner.

I got hit with an inspiration, and I wondered why I hadn't thought of it before. "Well, yes sir. The only other guy on the team who lives out this way is Johnny Zwicki. I'm sure I could catch a ride with him, as soon as he gets his license back." I didn't want to overplay my hand.

Mother's ears pricked up. "Zwicki? Isn't that the boy the highway patrol caught running whiskey last summer? Is that why he doesn't have a license? That boy's as wild as a March hare, all those Zwickis are. I'd just as soon you didn't ride with that wild child."

I gave one of those look-off-to-the-left half shrugs that signals defeat. It was so fake it actually made Daddy laugh.

"All right, Jack. We've been thinking this over. Your mother and I will get you that motor scooter. You are a good fellow, and I expect you to be a man when we give you a man's gift. When my father gave me my horse he told me, 'Never ride it hard and put it away wet.' Same goes for you and your Eagle. I expect it to be spotless, and you will be responsible for buying the gas and oil. You can keep it out in the barn with my pickup. I like that it's called Eagle. That's an important animal to us Creeks. Have you thought of a name for it yet?"

I was still in swoon gear, like a man who just won the Irish Sweepstakes, and could barely hear, much less think. "No sir, what do you think I ought to call it?"

He leaned back in his chair. "What about Tafah? That means feather in Creek. So you'd have an eagle feather. Very powerful medicine."

"Don't make me say 'He'll need it.' It's too obvious," Mother groused in her flat Missouri twang. I could tell she'd been out-voted.

My Eagle was hunter green with a tan saddle and a tan seat behind mine for a second rider. And I knew just who that second rider should be—Glinda Ewing.

Glinda and I had been dating off and on for about a year, but it was hard when you didn't have any wheels. We'd meet at the movie theater usually and watch a double feature while I methodically, glacially, moved my hand from her shoulder down the front of her sweater. It was slow and tedious work, but worth it. Glinda had—what was it Old Bob Hogan said about Jane Russell?—mezzanine majesty.

All of us guys had been watching Glinda building her mezzanine since eighth grade. Like a graceful athlete who seems almost casual about his talents, Glinda seemed to ignore her knockers, which made her all the more alluring. But when she got on the back of my Eagle and grabbed me tightly around the waist, both of us were acutely aware of her firm breasts pushing against my back. And both of us knew it was only a matter of time before we did something about it.

It happened one afternoon after we had just lost to Duncan three to two. I had pitched the first four innings and done okay, but I'd struck out twice, once with a guy on second, and I was feeling like I had let the team down.

As we were walking across the park to my motorbike, Glinda gave my hand an extra squeeze. "What do you say we go over to my house and study? My mother's gone to book club and it'll be real quiet."

I was still in a dark mood. "I don't know. I didn't even bring anything to study."

She pulled herself so close her lips were actually touching my ear. "That's all right, hon. I've got a couple of things for you to study, just as long as you want. And then maybe I'll do a little studying on my own."

After that we went steady all through the summer and fall. We'd take Tafah out to Lake Murray swimming and water skiing, go to the Carnegie library where Glinda would draw while I read books, and we'd travel to all the little towns in the area where I'd play American Legion summer league ball. Glinda would sit on the end of the bench and draw women in dresses and coats and stuff she'd design herself. She was real good. And we'd make love.

Glinda was a god-send to me, because Mother just kept getting sicker and sicker. Her cough got so bad in the fall that she broke a rib and got pleurisy. But she refused to stop smoking, even got defiant about it. Then sometime after Christmas my senior year she started going in and out of the hospital.

Everybody thought it was pneumonia at first, but long before the doctors told us, Daddy and I knew it was cancer. You could see it in her eyes.

You read obituaries about people dying of cancer and it's always "died after a long battle with cancer" or "died after a lengthy and valiant struggle with cancer." And here's the crazy part: my mother, who battled corrupt county commissioners, liars in Washington and Oklahoma City, dumb city ordinances and Republicans, didn't put up much of a fight against lung cancer. She'd read, smoke cigarettes and look out the window.

I didn't understand this, and rather than try to understand, I just got angry. This was the first time in my life when I could see plainly an ending that I both categorically rejected and was unable to alter. I felt like I needed to blame someone—the doctors, the cigarette companies, God. How could a world be so dumb to call them coffin nails and make songs about smoking yourself to death, and still sell them?

Finally, of course, I started blaming Mother for her own death. One February day I walked into her hospital room and found her, the oxygen tent thrown back, her blue feet dangling off the bed, smoking a Pall Mall. I became furious and raced to the bed table where I grabbed the pack and crushed it. She didn't move, just stared at me like she was watching a movie. I wanted to hit her; I wanted to hug her; I wanted to tell her I loved her, which I had never really done when it counted.

But I did none of those. I just stood in front of her and screamed. "These fucking cigarettes. These fucking cigarettes. These fucking cigarettes." Then came the tears and I ran out of the room.

I got on the Eagle and took off, not knowing or caring exactly where. Then I decided I'd go see Glinda. Maybe we'd run away and get married. Or maybe I'd take her to the Camelot Motel and just fuck her forever. Or maybe I'd slap the shit out of her because I knew she smoked Kools sometimes.

It wasn't such a bad day for February in Oklahoma, as I remember. It was all gray and brown and overcast, but most of the snow from the week before had melted, and the streets were dry. I still had a few angry tears when I hit the D Street hill way too fast. At the bottom of the hill, about a block from Glinda's, I hit a patch of black ice. My back wheel spun to the right and everything went into slow motion. I wasn't afraid and it seemed like I had all the time in the world to make decisions. I knew you weren't supposed to brake, so I gunned it in the direction of the slide, just like I'd been taught. For a second I thought I had it under control, then my front wheel hit a manhole cover and I flew over the handlebars. Even then, I thought I might be okay until I hit the stop sign about halfway up.

Years later when I met Che Guevara for the first time in my current rubber tree Nicaraguan home away from home, we got drunk on *Flor de Caña* rum and he told me about his buddy and him travelling all over South America on their motorcycles. "That was a magic motorbike and a magic trip," he said. "It changed everything for me."

That's when I told him about Tafah. "Talk about magic," I boasted through a thin veil of rum, "That motorcycle got me a lover, got me out of the army and brought me all the way from Oklahoma to Costa Rica."

"That must have been some bike," Che agreed, and took a long pull on his cigar.

CHAPTER 4

I broke my pelvis, my femur (thighbone, Old Bob, thighbone!) and my kneecap. The femur was so badly broken they had to put a steel rod in it. I was in a cast from my waist to my ankle for almost three months. This took care of baseball (forever, although I didn't know that at the time) and athletic scholarship offers from the University of Texas and Arizona State vanished overnight. So did the scout from Albuquerque.

I deeply regretted having to go to Mother's funeral in a wheelchair with my leg sticking straight out. But at least we didn't have to sit through one of those interminable sermons you usually get. Mother never was very churchy, so Old Bob and Mrs. Gibbs, who was the owner of the *Ardmorite,* rented the civic auditorium for the memorial.

It was a beautiful spring day and there was a pretty big turnout, including a lot of Daddy's Indian side of the family, which was a little surprising, because Creeks don't like to hang around dead people. Daddy promised them that it would just be talking, and the body wouldn't even be there, so they said okay, she was a good woman.

That being an election year, wherever there was a crowd, the politicians showed up like a pack of junk yard dogs. Governor Murray was there, of course. The same guy who had called her a Commie Pinko the year before now called Mother "one of the pioneering women journalists of this state." This hypocrisy infuriated me, and if you're starting to get the idea I was angry a lot in those days, you've just won a kewpie doll.

After the service, Daddy drove me home in the silent pickup and then took me out to the barn. "Take a look," he said quietly. There was my Eagle, completely restored. This made me a little angry, too, I'm ashamed now to say.

"Never thought I'd see that piece of shit again," I grumbled. "Just throwing good money after bad, if you ask me."

Daddy walked over and put his hand on the Cushman. "Guess that's why I didn't ask you, Jack. You're mad at everything and everybody right now and I can understand that. But you don't shoot a horse just because it threw you. Chances are by the time you get your cast off, you'll have outgrown old Tafah here, but that's not his fault. Maybe I'll just throw a tarp over it and save it for my grandchildren." He chuckled. "But I think I speak for Glinda's dad when I say you can take all the time you want in that department. We're in no hurry."

My eyebrows shot up in surprise, and my caught-in-the-act expression made us both laugh—my first laugh in weeks. I picked a non-existent thread off my plaster cast. "I'm not ready for that conversation just yet. Mind if I ask you something?"

"Shoot." He repeated the standing family joke. "I'm as smart as I want to be."

"Well, that's the point. I'm not. Not by half. College is just around the corner and some things have changed."

Daddy walked over and sat beside me on the hay bale which had replaced the despised wheelchair, at least for a while. He put his arm around my shoulder. "Yeah, I know all about the baseball scholarships drying up. Your mother and I talked about it. It doesn't matter, son. We've got a few bucks stashed away, and with your grades, you can go just about anywhere, I imagine."

"Thanks, Daddy. I'm thinking University of Oklahoma. What do you think?"

"Your mother and I talked about this, too, talked a lot. And for one of the few times in our lives, we found ourselves on opposite sides of the street. Beth thought you had the stuff to aim high—maybe Princeton or Yale, even Harvard. She said if you majored in—what do they call it these days?—Native American studies, Harvard would take you in a heartbeat. But I don't know. I hope you are proud of your Indian blood, and I'd love to see you learn Indian ways. I'll help you any way I can. But getting a degree in Indian? What the hell does anybody do with a degree in Indian? Go to work for the Bureau of Indian Affairs?" He gave a sound that was part laugh, part cough. "You know if you ever went to work for the BIA, as much as I love you, I'd have to track you down and shoot you."

I stared at him incredulously. "You called Mother Beth?"

* * *

My lingering foul mood, self-pity and contempt soon had an accompanying odor. As the weeks drug on and the weather grew warmer, a swampy fragrance rose out of my cast that all the talcum powder in the world couldn't mask.

The doctors told me that under no circumstance was I to get the plaster wet, so I was stuck. I actually tried rubbing Mum between my legs but it just made everything greasy and smell like a Mexican whorehouse. Glinda said it didn't matter, but she started coming over less and less.

Years later scuttling along a jungle path just above San Isidro, I experienced a *déjà vu* that only a smell can stimulate. We had just finished a baseball game where the other team had spent the afternoon throwing at my head as usual, and I was tired and trying to get home before dark. I never saw the vine and went flying headfirst into a wet, rotting pile of dead leaves and god-knows-what. The fetid jungle breath lurking just under the dried foliage smelled so much like my randy high school crotch that I just laid there, breathing it all in and laughing. The odorous symbolism of being caged in my body-cast cell and then being a self-imposed prisoner in that Stygian jungle seemed so convenient, so contrived I had to ask Carlos if he smelled it, too. "Yes," he said. "It's very ugly. It smells like dead dogs in the rain."

* * *

Second semester senior year was so full of nonsense, with yearbook signings and senior class talents shows and crap, I was about the only senior getting educated, and I was being home schooled. Old Bob Hogan took it on himself to not only continue our grammar and literary studies, he sent them flying off in different directions—Laurence Durrell, Thomas Mann, H.L. Mencken. Knowing my secret love of the *New Yorker*, he introduced me to the writers of the Algonquin Roundtable—Robert

Sherwood, George S. Kaufman, Marc Connelly, Dorothy Parker, who else?—Robert Benchley. And James Thurber (although I don't think he was a regular). Damn, we loved James Thurber.

One day we were sitting on the front porch reading the story of one of Thurber's hen-pecking Harridans out loud and laughing so hard Daddy stuck his head around the corner to make sure Old Bob hadn't declared an early start to happy hour.

I was sitting sideways on the glider, which was the only way I could sit. "You ever been married, Old Bob?" I asked idly.

"Oh, hell yes. How do you think I got these false teeth? Wife number one kicked my teeth in; wife number two tried to steal my new choppers along with everything else. Both good old gals by the way, in their fashion. How about you? I understand you've been dipping your wick in that Ewing girl. Any wedding bells in your future?"

"How poetic. Jesus, why don't I just take out a full-page ad? No, thanks to the fact that everybody in town seems to know more about my love life than I do, Glinda's father has decided to send her off to Sophie Newcomb in New Orleans. She's going to live with an aunt down there. And there's absolutely no way I'm going to Tulane. I'll probably go to OU. It's cheap, it's close and they have to take me."

"Anybody would take you, Jackson, but you better get on your horse and apply or you'll wind up at my alma mater—UHK." Old Bob noticed my furrowed brow. "That's the University of Hard Knocks. Lots of us graduated from there in the thirties. But the University of Oklahoma is a good choice. They've got a top-notch journalism school. Is that what you want to do? I figured as much as you hang around the paper, you ought to get paid for it."

"I do like the newspaper business, but no disrespect, instead of writing about current events, I think I'd like to make some. I'd like to get my law degree and go into politics. I've been thinking about this for years."

Old Bob leaned back in the white wicker rocker. "I guess you inherited more from your mother than the love of words, Jack. Politics was in her blood and she couldn't stand those pompous idiots in Oklahoma government who think that loud is the same thing as smart."

"I saw that last year when Mother debated Congressman Wickerman. What a dumbbell."

Old Bob leaned forward and fixed me with his gaze. "That's where you'd be wrong. Murray is a jackass, even he knows it. But Arthur Wickerman is a far different story. I know for a fact that he just makes up those Red-baiting statistics because they play good on radio and television. People are running scared, especially ever since Sputnik, and Wickerman is playing that like a finely-tuned violin. Congress is just a way-station for him; he's got his eye on a bigger prize. Don't sell Wickerman short; he's dangerous, not dumb. And one of these days, I'm going to get him . . . before he gets me."

CHAPTER 5

I had a high school teacher once who said "Show Jack Harjo a grain and he'll go against it."

Fair enough, and to my surprise and delight, the University of Oklahoma proved a fertile garden for me and hundreds of other contrarians, misfits, eccentrics and refuseniks I never knew existed and couldn't get enough of.

Students and fellow-travelers young and old came filing into Norman from every direction, economic level and educational achievement. A lot of them didn't hang around long, but it made for an amazing stew.

For one thing, OU in those days was almost comically inexpensive and easy to get into. If you were a resident of Oklahoma, all you had to do was show a high school diploma and a pulse, and you were in. And at six bucks an hour, you could scratch that itch to go to college for less than a hundred dollars a semester, which was about as smart as some people wanted to be.

Somewhere on the other side of the rubber plantation I can hear a guitar right now, being played pretty good, too, and it reminds me of an old buddy who I thought was one of those guys who just wanted to stick his toe in the academic waters—Leroy Goss from Idabel. Leroy and I had desks across from each other in Philosophy I first semester freshman year and I liked his down-home honesty. Leroy was as country as they come, with big, warty hands that gripped a guitar neck the way I'd grab a pencil. He'd sit out on the steps of Cameron Hall before class and just play the hell out of that guitar. And not just country music, either. If he wanted to play like Chet Atkins, he played like Chet Atkins. If he wanted to play like Chuck Berry, he played like Chuck Berry. I imagine he could have played like Segovia, too, if you had gotten him a record to listen to. Leroy couldn't read music; he wasn't all that good at reading, period. Leroy was the first person I ever met who convinced me there must be at least three or four kinds of brains. Around guitars and cars, you couldn't beat him. But for the stuff we were getting in class, he just sort of waded through it in a fog of wonder.

One day in November our philosophy professor told us that Rabbi Levinson would be guest lecturer next week to discuss the teachings of Moses Maimonides. Leroy leaned over to me and punched my arm in obvious pleasure. "Isn't college great?" he stage-whispered. "I didn't even know he *had* a last name."

Just as Leroy was a stranger academically, I became something of a social castaway. My attraction to the bohemian crowd at Norman was only partly self-inflicted. This surprised me at first, because the idea of being a couple of rungs down the social ladder had never even occurred to me in high school. I was popular without thinking about it; girls, letter jackets, good grades were all lined up like those little clay pipes in a shooting gallery. My occasional harangues in class were not only tolerated by my teachers, I think they sort of expected them. Just Jack being Jack, or maybe Jack being Jack's mother.

So when I got to OU I tried to fit in at first, but the world and I had been butting heads for six months and neither was in the mood to yield.

Some of my friends from Ardmore were joining fraternities, so I thought what the hell, me too. I pledged Delta Tau, which secretly wasn't my first choice, and I think from the start I must have been giving off vapors of alienation. I went to all the pledge meetings and did my weekly chores but I just couldn't keep my mouth shut. I kept piling up demerits to the point that some of the seniors didn't even bother to learn my name, and just shook their heads when they saw me. In the curious language of the Greek system, I got "depledged" during hell week for refusing to wear a pound of liver strung around my neck under my shirt for five days. Quoting e. e. cummings' "I Sing of Olaf Glad and Big," I shouted "There is some shit I will not eat," and became a former Delta Tau before the words had reverberated down the hall to the house mother's apartment. Curiously, I would run into the fraternity-speak of "depledging" again in Peace Corps training, where volunteers were getting "deselected" left and right. There's a thread there somewhere, but it's too hot to figure it out.

* * *

Second semester my freshman year I ran into another bad patch, this one academic. I flunked Spanish I, if you can fucking believe that. I also flunked ROTC, which surprised no one and made me something of a hero among the geeks and freaks I was increasingly hanging out with. I also aced my advanced English and American history, making me, according to my mostly-neglected dorm counselor, perhaps the first C student in OU history never to get a C. The university put me on academic probation just on general principles and, I think, so they could send a righteously-indignant letter to Daddy full of phrases like "not meeting agreed-upon expectations," "excessive absences," and my favorite, "only cadet in ROTC never to have cleaned his weapon."

This had far less impact on Daddy than the office of the registrar might have expected, but it did occasion his coming to Norman.

Sitting over our Theta burgers at the Town Tavern one Saturday, our conversation began where most of them did—way over in the farthest reaches of the outfield, talking about sports.

"Did you see where Dale Long hit seven home runs in seven consecutive games?" Daddy asked, sticking some cheddar cheese back inside the bun with a finger. "That's something. Keeps that up, he'll break Ruth's record before the fourth of July. You gonna go out for the baseball team?"

I was used to this slow way Daddy had of sidling up to the real subject. It was like I was a ten-pound bass and he was playing me, bringing me in slowly, giving me my head.

"Not this year," I said to my burger. "I thought I'd play a little American Legion ball this summer, then maybe give it a shot next spring." I finally raised my head and looked Daddy in the eye, ready to take my punishment. "I can't try out until next year anyway, because they put me on probation. Did you get the letter from the dean?"

"Yeah, kind of stuffy, wasn't it? But I guess they got their rules, just the same as everybody else. And you broke a bunch of them. Now listen up,

Jack. I'm not mad at you. But I am disappointed. Your mother thought you could be the best college student ever, and I still do. But if you don't think so, quit. The pickup's outside; you're welcome home. Get a job on the paper, go to work in the oil fields, run away and join the circus, I don't give a darn. But Jack, don't you dare be average, bumping along making an A over here and an F over there. Frankly, average is the name of the road I went down, and if it hadn't of been for Beth, I wouldn't have amounted to a hill of beans." He paused and smiled that toothy dazzler. "Well, maybe oily beans. But you've got it in you to be as good as your mother predicted. Make your mother proud, son. Fish or cut bait."

"I need to pick my fights a little better, don't I?" I asked, addressing my French fries this time. "I'll fish."

* * *

To belabor the metaphor, I may have decided to fish but that summer there was still a lot of bait to cut.

Glinda had come back from Sophie Newcomb at least ten years older, with no apparent knowledge of her former life. I heard that she had gotten pinned to a halfback from Tulane named Ravenoux or something like that. She'd already been back in Ardmore a week when I ran into her at The Vogue, as I was helping get stuff for Art's Pepper Holiday column. She gave me a peck on the cheek and suggested we get together sometime. Well, it wasn't unexpected and it was fun while it lasted. But it was what newspapermen call a sidebar. It was baseball, one of my Big Three, which was the lead.

And my personal lead story that summer was a stunner, at least to me. I had decided I wanted to get back to American Legion baseball. I knew I was slightly damaged goods, but I frankly thought most teams would still want me. I wanted to play the hero, so one day I dropped in on Mr. James, the store manager of the Oklahoma Tire, Auto and Building Supply Company, which they mercifully shortened to OTABCO. His team was in last place in the American Legion Sooner League, and even though I was having a little trouble going to my left, I thought I might catch on at first base. Mr. James had wanted me to play for him bad two summers ago, so I asked for a tryout.

We went down the next morning to the cluster of ball fields at Will Rogers Park. My tryout started out okay. I could still hit with power, but when I tried to leg out a couple of grounders, I was a half a step slower than my junior year. And that half a step was the difference between being on the team and being in the band.

Everybody could see that I wasn't the same Jack Harjo, and the usual infield chatter got as quiet as a funeral home. The silence went through me like a knife. Nevertheless I trotted back to Mr. James, who had been sitting behind the backstop in one of those folding canvas director's chairs, which for a man his size was tempting fate.

"What do you think, Mr. James? I really think I can help OTABCO out this summer, and I'm working hard on getting back in shape. I'm left-handed; I could do first base. I think I can help the team."

The big man moved his cigar from one side of his mouth to the other. "Harjo, I've known you since you were in sixth grade, so I'm not going to start lying to you now. You run to first base like Walter Brennan. You might get faster; you might not." He put his arm on my shoulder just as I was mounting a defense in my mind. "Now hold on, son. That doesn't mean I can't use you. I've seen you play. You know your baseball. Look, our team manager has just been transferred to our Tulsa store. How would you like to be the new manager of the Treaders? If anybody could lead us out of the basement, it's you. And there's fifty bucks a month in it. What do you say?"

I was hit with a wave of nausea so strong I could taste the acid in the back of my throat. I opened my mouth to say "Not on your life," but for some reason it came out "I'll take it."

Although I never lost my rolling gait, I did get faster. And learning to be a manager would serve me well later in Costa Rica.

CHAPTER

6

One high-dust August afternoon my American Legion OTABCO Treaders were playing the Conoco Oilers in the little town of Lone Grove a few miles down the road from our farm when I heard a familiar voice.

"Damn, Jack, you don't stay in one place much, do you?"

"Leroy Goss," I shouted and grabbed his big knobby hand. "What are you doing this far from Idabel?"

"Oh, I'm roustabouting this summer over at Healdton. Making good money just sitting on a well and cutting weeds. But you know what the best thing is about working in the oil fields? It teaches you stuff. It teaches you to get your sorry ass back to college and stop riding a sling blade."

"Leroy, no offense, but I just never figured you for the college type. Didn't I hear you flunked out?"

"Well, as a matter of actual fact, I did. But I'm thinking of taking another run at it. And that's why I looked you up. You are loaded with smarts, and I figure with you riding shotgun I got a better than average chance. How would you like to be roommates? I'm not coming with my hat in my hand on this thing. I've already got an apartment lined up, it's got its own kitchen and everything, and I put the first month's rent down as a deposit. I'll be willing to eat that if you'll help me with English and stuff. You're good for me, Jack. Philosophy was one of the few courses I passed last year."

So I quit cutting bait, went fishing and took Leroy along with me.

The name of our scruffy apartment building was Los Dones, pronounced *donaze* and which loosely translates to The Gentlemen. Most people called it the Alamo, because it was white adobe and, as one of the residents Zelda told us, was where outmatched students took their last stand.

The apartments were built hacienda-style around an abandoned fish pond. In the two years I lived there, the only thing that was ever in that pond was Larry Reznick's Nash Rambler. In one of those moments of whisky lucidity, I bet him that the Rambler wouldn't fit between the two white stucco pillars that guarded the courtyard. He took the bet, took another swig of Jack Daniels and to my amazement, hurtled effortlessly, like the biblical camel through the eye of the needle, into the moonlit courtyard. But he had less than fifteen feet to come to a stop, and he didn't. His little car hit the raised tiles lining the pond, bucked and dove into the abyss. The Rambler came to rest with its nose in the pond and its trunk pointing skyward. And in another predicament that defied the laws of physics, Larry discovered that the pond was so narrow he couldn't open either door.

"Call a tow truck," he wailed. "I'm stuck in here."

"Good idea," I said with slurred dignity. "Just give me the phone number of someone stupid enough to send a tow truck to pluck a drunk out of a fish pond at two in the morning. Roll down both windows and go to sleep, Larry. We'll start fresh after breakfast. Well, at least I'll have breakfast."

When the guy from the Deep Rock service station got there the next day, he had to take off one of the fenders to get the car back onto the street. It took him two hours. Larry snored his way through the whole thing.

Larry Reznick was one of The Gentlemen, our next door neighbor, as it turned out. And he was typical of the flawed, funny and unforgettable neighbors who would shape my life.

I quickly came to think of Los Dones as not so much an apartment complex, as one of those screwball Preston Sturges movies from the thirties. The only things we lacked were Monty Woolley and a tiger on a leash.

So here's Los Dones The Movie, and its wondrous cast of characters:

Larry Reznick. Due to a loophole Larry had discovered in his late father's trust fund, Larry was "a seventh-year junior majoring in absolutely everything." Much to the displeasure of his gorgeous and only slightly-older step-mother, Larry received $10,000 a year from daddy's trust until he turned thirty or for as long as he stayed in college. So every year or so, he'd change majors, lose a ton of credit hours, go to class and cash checks. When I met him his majors had already included comparative religions, pharmacy, English, library science and American history (pre-Civil War). He was currently in Latin American studies and was casting an eye toward anthropology. "Then there's pre-med, law school, maybe even a doctor of divinity. So many books, so much time." He was also, I found out, minoring in grass.

Tiger Moran. Tiger was the handyman and super who lived rent-free in the back apartment near the alley in exchange for fixing toilets and changing light bulbs. He had once been a bantam-weight club fighter in Mexico and south Texas under the name of Chico "El Tigre" Moreno. He had taken way too many shots to the head and had a nose that went left when the rest of him was going straight ahead. One look at his face and you didn't have to ask how cauliflower ears got their name. But even though he looked like a thug, he had the gentlest eyes, and a soul to match.

It took me months to finally be invited into Tiger's apartment, and when I got there I discovered that every square inch of wall space was covered in Tiger's paintings. Other people had mentioned Tiger's art work to me and made fun of it, but once you really looked at his pieces they stuck in your dream memories forever. He painted on everything—plywood, canvas when he could afford it, burlap sacks, painted-over pictures that past renters had left when they moved, sides of packing boxes, old license plates, the backs of movie posters he got from the Boomer Theater. His pictures were very colorful, like some of the art from Haiti that I saw when I moved to Central America. His primitive scenes had no sense of perspective, so chickens and automobiles might be the same size. And the pictures were intricate, exotic things that were filled with flowers, unicorns, dead bodies, angels, birds and eyeballs. One time I gave him ten dollars and a canvas and asked him to paint me a picture for the apartment. He said he would, but a month later he sheepishly told me that he couldn't get rid of it; it would be like selling a baby. He added that I could come visit the painting whenever I wanted, and he was sorry but he'd spent the ten dollars.

Zelda. Zelda, who had buried her last name along with her past, was a teaching assistant in the English department. Her specialty was Spencer's "The Faerie Queene," and outside of Old Bob Hogan, she was the best-read person I knew. She was also by far the most outrageous.

Zelda had plenty of time to catch up on her reading. She was part-owner (with Nigel Branson, who I'll get to in a minute) and manager of Lady Chatterley's Book Store. Zelda became something of a campus celebrity by periodically being hauled in by the local cops for selling dirty books. It was a fantastic marketing ploy, and Nigel cheerfully paid her fine, then slipped her copies of "Tropic of Cancer," which he got from his uncle in Australia.

Zelda was as over the top as her bookstore, and along the same lines. Her desire to shock equaled her unquenchable sexual appetite, and at all hours of the afternoons and evenings you'd hear her screaming orgasms mixed in with her constant Edith Piaf records. She kept the windows open just in case you weren't paying attention.

Zelda was also a very caring and generous friend, willing to fix you dinner or lend you money. "I just can't figure you out," I admitted to her one afternoon.

"Just think of me as the big sister you never had," she laughed. "The one who likes to fuck."

Nigel and Mari Branson. Although they both came from Australia, they came from such opposite ends of the social continuum, I think it even surprised them that they had met in the middle. Nigel was a beefy-faced blond bear with an accent so far from Oklahoma, it took me the better part of a month to figure out what he was saying. This caused some confusion, because Nigel never shut up. He'd tell a story with a punch line that flew right over my head, give me a wink and a good-natured elbow in the ribs and roar with laughter at his own joke.

Nigel and Mari didn't so much come to America as escape to it. Mari was, in the words of Nigel, "my ever-lovin' Abo." She was the first woman I had ever met with a tattoo, and it was on the left side of her face. She was the only aborigine I ever met, and although her face looked like a warrior from another planet, her soft accent came from the same twangy outback station as Nigel.

Both Mari and Nigel were getting their masters in fine arts; he in drama, she in sculpting, primarily ceramics and pottery. Their apartment was the off-campus headquarters of half the fine arts department it seemed, and people flooded in and out of there all day. One of the attractions was the Branson Bushman Never-ending Stew. This was a giant iron pot of stew that stood simmering, morning and night, seven days a week. Next to the stove was a big stack of bowls and spoons that came mostly from the thrift shop, and some from Mari's potter's wheel. Over the stove there was a big carefully hand-drawn sign on the wall that read "Bushman Stew—It's Really Up to You. Bring What You Can, Take What You Want." People would come in with carrots, potatoes, onions or celery and add them to the concoction. Nigel would add chunks of beef from time to time. Next to the big sign was a smaller sign that read "No Beets." Below that someone had scrawled "Or Okra," and under that was a small pencil addendum, "Too late."

"This is absolutely delicious," Larry told me one day. "But do you realize there are bits of this stew that must be a couple of years old?"

"No worries," Nigel bellowed as he overheard. "Mari starts a new batch every New Year's Day."

General Tom. Tom was an entrepreneur, self-appointed head of Los Dones and the man who gave me my start in journalism, in a way. There were other tenants at Los Dones from time to time, like the Iranian geology students who stayed up all night playing cards and kept so much to themselves we weren't sure how many of them they were; and the older man from Bombay whose English vocabulary was better than mine, but whose accent was an easy target for Nigel's spot-on mimicry. Nigel's ability to nail the Indian's speech pattern was hilarious to Nigel, amusing to us, but so murderously serious to Mr. Chatterjee that he moved out rather than face further humiliation. He left a basket of beets at Nigel and Mari's front door with a note suggesting that Nigel might want to consider drinking poison and going directly to hell. But none of the occupants had the immediate and permanent impact of General Tom.

Tom Wilson may have lived in The Gentlemen, but he was no gentleman. He was no general either, for that matter. He was a scalawag, an absolute charmer whose cherubic face was catnip to women and side-kick friendly to men. Unlike Zelda who hid her past, Tom paraded his, re-invented and re-imagined to suit his audience or just for the hell of it. He was the owner of General Tom's Pizza Palace, a hole-in-the-wall take-out pizza parlor that he claimed he won in a poker game (the truth jury is still out on that one). He was cheerful, hard-working, constantly in love, constantly broke (one time he told me that he had been created solely as a way for money to travel from one place to another) and with almost daily get-rich ideas that usually involved schemes just two or three clicks off moral center.

General Tom served as the bridge between my apartment life and my other new-found love, journalism school. I slept at Los Dones, but I lived at the j-school. Of course, I knew the newspaper business already, and I quickly settled in as a reporter on the campus daily. But there was so much more—a dazzling array of courses in advertising and public relations, photojournalism and radio and television production. They even had their own radio station. That's all I ever talked about, I guess, and one night, more to shut me up than anything else, I think, General Tom made me a proposition.

"Jack, you are clearly a man on the make in this journalism deal, and I'm just the man who can help you get to the top of the heap. You can even help me out a little in the process. We got all this rebel yell nonsense going on with the pizza boxes and such (before Tom bought/won it, the place had been called General Lee's Southern Pizza, which made no sense to anybody) and I'm thinking of a make-over. How would you like to be my director of advertising and marketing? There's no money in it of course. I don't want to jeopardize your amateur standing. But think of the resume, think of the prestige, think of the free pizza."

Like a lot of young people, I didn't exactly know when to shut up and just say yes. "Well, actually, I do have some experience in retail advertising. You may have seen my ads for McCall's Restaurant for their Sooner Nooner Eighty-Niner? That was their eighty-nine cent blue plate special. It was pretty popular."

"Yeah," General Tom said a little absently, "That was the clincher for me. Okay, you've got a job. Now put your thinking cap on."

About a month later I came running back from the j-school one night with the biggest idea of my entire life. Everybody was sitting around the dry pond eating pizza that General Tom often brought back after closing. Larry and Zelda were sharing a joint and a beer. Leroy was playing and singing some of the protest songs Zelda had taught him like "Joe Hill," "I Shall Not Be Moved," and "Oh, Freedom." Leroy and his guitar fit right into the Los Dones crowd because of his incredible ability to hear a song once and play it. When he found out Woody Guthrie used to live in Okemah, he was hooked on protest songs (with Zelda's occasional afternoon urgings).

"Welcome home, Harjo," General Tom said, handing me a doobie, which I refused. I didn't smoke in those days. "Got me that million-dollar idea yet?"

"Actually yes," I semi-shouted and everybody stopped and looked at me just as I had daydreamed it jogging across campus. "General, when do people eat pizza?"

"Nigel and I eat it cold for breakfast," Tom said, "But I doubt that catches on. Most folks like it for dinner."

"Well, I've been doing a survey for my marketing class. Most college kids like it as their *second* dinner. They eat dinner in the dorms or fraternities at six and by ten they're starving. They're starving for pizza. When do you close?"

"We close at ten," General Tom said slowly, his eyebrow arching as light bulbs started going off in his brain.

"Okay, I want you to stay open till midnight. You'll be the only place open that late except that greasy spoon Mexican place down by the railroad station, and they don't deliver. And every night we'll remind the entire university how hungry they are and how good your pizzas are. We're going to have our own radio show, starting at ten when the air time is dirt cheap. We'll play jazz, comedy records, Hoyt Axton, Pete Seeger—stuff you can't hear on regular radio. And every now and then we'll give away a pizza. I even got a name for the show. Ready? 'General Tom's Radio Free Pizza Hour.' The pizza boxes will have pizzas dropping out of airplanes like Care packages. What do you think?"

"I was thinking about holding off for the Sooner Nooner, but I guess that's more Zelda's department. Let's do it Harjo. I'll get rich and you'll get famous."

CHAPTER

7

On March 7, 1960 the university radio station KNOU ("you're in the know with KNOU") debuted the Radio Free Pizza Hour amid as much hype as I could think of. Weeks before the show went on the air, we sent letters to all the Greek houses asking them to submit a pizza recipe that would be named for their fraternity or sorority. The winner was to get ten free pizzas delivered to their door every Friday for a month. To our surprise, twenty-eight out of the thirty-six houses on campus responded. When we announced the first winner (Kappa Sig with their Fiji Island Pizza covered in ham and pineapple) General Tom's delivered more pizza in two hours than they had ever done in an entire night.

I was the show's emcee, General Tom was my wise-cracking and slightly racy alter-ego, and Nigel would come in from time to time with his incredible and often hilarious ability to mimic anyone. The show really caught fire and soon I developed an audience, a growing reputation at the j-school and one very powerful and life-long enemy.

* * *

I wasn't the only one learning how to use the media. United States Congressman Arthur Wickerman became an early adapter. Because he was never really in favor of anything, just against stuff, he found that his messages were particularly well-suited for radio and television. While his poor opponents were diligently writing editorials and explaining their position to garden clubs, Wickerman would stare directly into the camera, wave his left finger in the air, and in his sing-song delivery announce "My name is Arthur Wickerman, and I WANT TO WORK FOR YOU."

Wickerman's red-baiting, commie-in-every-corner message was especially effective on radio, where he could slip and slide around any real facts or figures. "How many communists and socialists are hiding behind our ivy-covered university walls, ladies and gentlemen? How many professors are using your tax dollars to teach Marxist-Leninist dribble? I think you would be amazed. I certainly was. My congressional investigation of socialists in the classroom is starting to hit mighty close to home, yes mighty close, and I need you to return me to congress to finish this job. It won't be an easy job; the price of freedom is eternal vigilance. But it's a job I intend to do, because I'm Arthur Wickerman and I WANT TO WORK FOR YOU."

Wickerman's successful anti-communist campaign was a little surprising to some political pundits outside the state. After Senator McCarthy's famous flame-out on television, and the movie-star communist witch hunt of the HUAC more or less sinking of its own weight, most politicians were scrambling to emulate the charismatic and enthusiastic Jack Kennedy. Even Nixon, who had cut his political eye-teeth chasing Commies, started talking about broad-brush issues like our place in the international community and this being the American Century. But Wickerman knew his Okies, and he was using Communism as code for Catholic. "We need congressmen and, yes, presidents, who will take their marching orders from the people, not Moscow or the Vatican."

Wickerman was one of the new breed of Southern Republicans. For years he had campaigned as a Dixiecrat, as he and his fellow conservative politicians called themselves. But the national Democratic Party had grown infuriated that he was going against message to tie Kennedy to the Pope and, not so subtly, Russia, and it stripped him of his powerful seat as chair of the House foreign relations committee. It surprised nobody that Wickerman and a dozen other congressmen from Texas and the South switched to the Republican Party for the 1960 elections.

This was fodder for newspapers across the country and rather than hurt Wickerman, it simply gave him another target. He went after newspapers with a vengeance, the *New York Times, Washington Post* and most of the syndicated columnists. But he didn't mind a fight in his own back yard, so the *Tulsa Tribune* and even my old friend the *Ardmorite* would get tarred with the congressman's "fellow traveler" brush. All you had to do was hint, as Old Bob Hogan did a few times, that a congressman should stand for *something*. "You'd think as often as he wields that oratorical hammer, Arthur Wickerman could build himself a platform," Old Bob wrote in an editorial. "He seems content to tear down the walls of academia."

"It's the hammer of justice," Wickerman responded, quoting Woody Guthrie for perhaps the only time in his life. "And this is one hammer that doesn't come with a sickle, as it appears to do in the editorial pages of the *Ardmorite*."

Well, all right, I figured, fair is fair. Go after Old Bob; get a piece of me. Although this was just a pipsqueak radio show on a campus radio station, Norman was in Wickerman's district. Most of the students still didn't have the vote, but pizza-loving seniors did and so did teaching assistants, faculty and the thousands of people who worked at the university and listened to jazz.

I knew I couldn't take him on toe-to-toe the way my mother might have; I had zero credibility. But I had seen him go nuts that time at Oklahoma City University when the audience laughed at him, so I knew that was his Achilles heel.

First, I sat down with Nigel with as many transcriptions of Wickerman spots, speeches and interviews as I could find. Nigel listened fiercely, jotting down favorite Wickerman words and platitudes, making tick marks over some words, diphthong swashes over others, and laughing, always laughing. Sometimes he'd jab his finger at the tape recorder in kind of a "see there?" motion.

In less than three evenings, Nigel nailed him. It seemed almost impossible for me to comprehend how his thick Aussie accent could completely disappear and be replaced by that arrogant sing-song twang I loved to hate.

So about midway through one Thursday night show, I announced to General Tom that we were pleased to have a very special guest visit our lavish underground studios (actually a former faculty office with no windows), the Honorable Arty Bickersham.

"Ladies and gentlemen, welcome to a new segment of our show, Open Mike with Open Minds. And what mind could possibly be more open, vacant even, than our first guest. Um, how would you prefer I address you, sir?"

"Well, son, when the Lord made me, he made a simple man; a man of the land and the oil that runs beneath it. Let's not stand on ceremony—'Your Congresship' will be just fine. I'd just as soon you didn't call me Governor . . . yet. Lord knows there are still weeds to be pulled from this garden before I take center stage among those derricks in Oklahoma City. So fire away, boy."

"Yes, your Congresship. I must say I'm a little surprised to see you here. Didn't you say last week that the University of Oklahoma is a hotbed of socialism?"

"Let's not beat around the bush. I said 'communism and socialism.' Why son, even your football team is called 'Big Red.' Coincidence? I don't think so. But I'm keeping an open mind because I am Arty Bickersham and I WANT TO WORK FOR YOU."

About twice a week Nigel/Arthur would show up with some funny, and occasionally quotable, stuff. His comments about the Soviet Olympic women runners having more beards than the House of David baseball team ran in the Oklahoma Press Association's monthly magazine, complete with a sidebar about Bickersham being a figment of the imagination of the Radio Free Pizza Hour. This in turn prompted a long piece about politics and college humor in the local Norman newspaper. The reporter got Wickerman to say that he had never heard our program, he never stayed up that late, but if somebody from the show wanted to get up at six am and come on the farm report, he'd be only too happy to have a chat. So of course, the next night Nigel pretended to show up with a chicken who he explained was his co-host on his morning show "You Bought the Farm."

One night after Nigel had reminded the audience that the price of freedom at General Tom's was $3.50 with extra cheese and your choice of two toppings, I slipped on the new Horace Silver album and settled in to listen.

The telephone rang. "Hello, Radio Free Pizza," I answered.

"Is this Jack Harjo?"

I looked quickly around the tiny studio, "Nigel, is that you?"

"No it isn't, you little shit. You know perfectly well who this is. So I see the rancid apple doesn't fall far from the tree. Commie mother; Commie son. Well, you and that whole nest of communists down at the *Ardmorite* have had your fun. But it doesn't pay to fuck with your superiors. Tell your friend Bob Hogan to tune into 'Oklahoma This Week' on channel four. You'll both get a big kick out of it, if you keep an open mind."

I called Old Bob the next morning to tell him about Arthur Wickerman's threat.

"I'm not surprised, Jackson," Old Bob said. "I told you a long time ago that I'd better get him before he gets me. Looks like I'm about to become the gitee. Tell you what. Why don't I come up to Norman this week-end and we can watch the program together. You can show me around campus and I can pretend I'm an alum. And I'll tell you all about what you're likely to hear Sunday before you get it directly from the horse's ass."

Three days later, I sat in stony silence in one of the dark booths in the Kettle, the only up-scale restaurant on campus corner. Old Bob looked over his iced tea at me with a mixture of compassion and pity.

"It's all true, Jack. For once Wickerman was telling the truth. When he said that we should be looking into Communists in the press, and a good place to start would be the editor of the *Daily Ardmorite*, he knew he had me. He's known my youthful indiscretion for years and was just waiting to cash the check.

"In 1935 I was dust-bowl broke, hungry and out of work. I'd been laid off at the Oklahoma City *Times*, and nobody was hiring. I didn't know a thing about oil wells, and I couldn't even get a job cutting wheat, cause there weren't any crops to speak of. I was a sports reporter at the *Times*, and about as politically savvy as a baseball glove. So when a guy named Lester Rodney told me they were starting a sports section in the *Daily Worker*, I applied for the job. I knew the *Daily Worker* was a Communist newspaper, but I couldn't figure how that would change the score of the Dodger games, and it didn't. Then one day, to impress a gal at the paper, like an idiot I joined the Communist Party. I only went to a few meetings, but the stain was on me.

"In 1942 I enlisted and served in Italy, mostly typing reports that nobody read. When I got out of the Army, I worked for a few years for *Stars and Stripes*, but in ten years Russia had gone from being an ally to being an enemy, and when the editor of *Stars and Stripes* found out I used to work for the *Daily Worker*, he said he was sorry, but he had no choice. Any other newspaper, maybe, he said, but not the *Stars and Stripes*.

"So I made my way back to Oklahoma and applied for a job on the *Ardmorite*. Mr. Gibbs was still alive in those days and he had been kind of a fiery La Follette progressive back in the twenties. He remembered my work at the *Times* and gave me a job. I thought it was all over, and good riddance. Then Walter Winchell published a list of *Daily Worker* editors and reporters in the New York *Post*, of all the damn places, and my name made the list. Probably the only person in Oklahoma to read the damn thing all the way through was a first-term congressman named Guess Who. He remembered my name from the *Times*, too, and tried to hold my past over my head like the sword of Damocles.

"Old man Gibbs wouldn't give Wickerman the time of day, and neither did Mrs. Gibbs. They stuck with me and stuck with your mother when Wickerman would make his annual appeal to get her fired. But this time is different.

"It's a television world out there, Jack, and Wickerman knows how to play it like a Stradivarius. When Wickerman reveals that I was in the communist party, it's going to put the knife in deep. More Oklahomans are going to watch Huntley—Brinkley tomorrow night than will read all the newspapers in the state combined. And they'll be watching *Oklahoma This Week,* too. I just can't put Mrs. Gibbs and all the guys through this. I was a member of the communist party, that's a tattoo on my soul, and every editorial I write from here on in will be suspect, or worse. So I've written my last editorial, Harjo. I'm heading up to Denver to look up a couple of old Army buddies in the airline business. Maybe I can catch on writing technical manuals and stuff."

He pulled an envelope out of his coat pocket and slid it across the table toward me.

"What's this?" I asked quietly.

"Aw, don't worry. It's not some hearts and flowers goodbye letter. I'm not made that way, and neither are you. That's a list of one hundred words you couldn't define with a pistol at your head. When I return in triumph a couple of years from now, I'm going to test you on every one of them. And thanks for lunch. If I'd of known you were buying, I'd of ordered steak."

* * *

Two weeks later I was pulling afternoon shift on the university newspaper, manning the Associated Press telex looking for stories that would interest college kids. We used to call it "rip and write."

I got a "one bell," which usually meant a story that would have local interest, if any at all. This one had all of that: "Robert S. Hogan, two-time winner of the Oklahoma Press Association Editor of the Year award, died this morning in a one-car accident on the Raton Pass in New Mexico. Hogan was the long-time editor of the Ardmore, Oklahoma, *Daily Ardmorite.* Recently he had admitted to allegations by US Representative Arthur Wickerman (R-Okla.) that he had once been a member of the communist party. Hogan apparently lost control of his automobile and crashed into a bridge abutment."

There was more to the story, but not a lot more. Old Bob couldn't even keep his dignity in death. I ripped the story off the machine, crumpled it up and threw it in the waste basket.

I asked my faculty advisor if I could read a eulogy to Old Bob that night on my show, and he agreed. But he said if there was even a passing mention of Wickerman, he'd pull the plug.

I agreed and lived up to my promise. I can't even remember exactly what I said that night, but it was from the heart and I tried as hard as I could to replace any anger with respect for a fallen comrade.

Exhausted and in no mood for banter, I sent everybody home, put on Miles Davis' *Kind of Blue* and sat staring at the wall.

There was a light tap on the door and a young woman entered. Lit from the hall behind her, she had a nimbus of unruly red hair that looked like it was staging a prison break. She had the whitest skin I'd ever seen and gigantic round horn-rimmed glasses that made her look very intelligent, very pretty and very East Coast.

"Hi," I said, coming half-way out of my chair. "If you've come for the Sing for Your Supper segment, that's not until tomorrow night, and it's down in the Student Union."

"No. I was just driving home and heard your wonderful tribute to Mr. Hogan. He must have meant a great deal to you. I'd like to offer my condolences."

"Thanks, but you don't have to do that."

"Actually, I feel very strongly that I do. You see, I think the man who may have been indirectly responsible for Mr. Hogan's death is my father. My name is Judy Wickerman.

CHAPTER 8

"Nimbus" was the fifty-third word on Old Bob's list. It means halo. I thought it meant cloud. I didn't use it just now to show off, just to raise a pencil toast to a good man. Can you believe a guy whose entire life is coming apart at the seams taking the time to write out a couple of year's worth of entries for our dictionary game? Me neither, and it haunted me.

I've still got the list—three creased and yellowing pages that I keep folded in a book of poetry by Ruben Dario. I keep them not because of their instructional value; I memorized all the words long ago. I keep them because Old Bob wrote them in long hand. It's kind of like a snapshot, I guess.

For the first few years I kept them because I was looking for clues, reading the words over and over trying to find a sign. And it's funny; the sign I was looking for was the sign I desperately hoped I'd never find. Did Old Bob send me a message? Did the words get darker, more ominous near the end? Did the handwriting get shakier as Four Roses became three, then one? What were you doing at Raton Pass that afternoon, Robert S. Hogan? Did you fall asleep at the wheel? Were you drunk? If you were really going to commit suicide, why did you talk about a triumphant return? It's a conundrum (word number 10).

The woman with the cloudy halo of red hair knew the definition of every damn one of the words on the list. Every one. I used to test her on them until it became clear it wasn't a test of her intelligence; it was a test of my humility.

Judy Wickerman was simply smarter than I was—Roger Wilco, over and out. She also became a major part of my life. But we almost never got beyond that first meeting at the radio station.

We didn't meet cute, as they say in the movies.

In the throes of my just-below-the-surface redskin rage, I was in no mood to talk to anybody, especially someone with a name like that. It was like going to American Bandstand and being introduced to your new dancing partner, Annette Hitler. Makes you want to sit the next one out. So I asked her to leave me alone.

"I understand," she said, shaking my hand firmly. "I probably wouldn't forgive me, either. But if you ever want to talk, I'm living over at Miss Hetty's. Give me a call sometime. I really like your show."

You don't pick your parents, of course, and as I thought about her that night (and I couldn't think of anything else), it occurred to me that maybe she wore her name like a penance, a hair shirt or a bed of nails. She said her name the way a person would take off her clothes and stand in front of you, defiant, naked and uncertain. By the time I finally finished walking around campus and got back to my apartment early the next morning, I was pretty certain I was in love with her.

Getting to see her was another matter entirely.

Miss Hetty's was the Oklahoma equivalent of New York City's Barbizon, a women's residence just a click above the YWCA. Most of the women at Miss Hetty's were graduate students or seniors who had outgrown the collective nonsense of sorority life. I naturally assumed, wrongly as it turned out, that Judy Wickerman was older than I. She certainly seemed more sophisticated.

Leroy and I didn't have a telephone and in fact telephones in and around the OU campus were about as plentiful as they are here at Che's camp. But since walking unannounced into Miss Hetty's was not something for the faint of heart, I called from the pay phone outside of Zelda's bookstore. Miss Hetty's only had one telephone, too, so you were just supposed to leave messages or arrange a place to meet. I couldn't leave a pay phone number to call back, and I didn't dare set up our first date by leaving a message, so I just said, "Please tell her Jack Harjo called and I'll call her back."

Eight days in a row I called, often twice a day. Finally the woman on the other end of the line said, "I don't know who you are, Jack Harjo, but you are one persistent son of a gun. I wish my boy friend showed as much gumption. This must be the fifth time I've taken a message from you. Judy said if you called to come down to the Kennedy for President headquarters. It's on Main Street. If you get there by noon, maybe you can take her out to lunch. And if she won't go with you, my name's Dianne, with an e. Just in case you're interested."

Kennedy for President headquarters? Arthur Wickerman's daughter? That must make for some pretty quiet family dinners, I figured.

I borrowed Leroy's old Plymouth and arrived one Saturday morning in June at 11:45. The building was the former Boomer Bank that had gone belly up the year before. The place was a maze of bridge tables and folding chairs with dozens of people, mostly pretty young women, writing post cards, stuffing envelopes, checking addresses, putting brochures, bumper stickers and lapel pins in boxes, drawing little circles and pushing pins in a big map leaning against an easel, and talking on more telephones than I'd ever seen in one place before. Some of the women, including Judy, were wearing straw hats, so I didn't pick her out until she stood and came striding toward me like Katherine Hepburn in "Pat and Mike." She was wearing a big campaign button that read "Jackie's Husband for President."

"Hello, Jack Harjo," she said, pinning an "All the Way with JFK" button on my shirt. "Thanks for being so persistent. Let's get something to eat. I'm so hungry I could eat a horse."

"Then you're in luck," I said, fingering my new button. "We'll go to Bob's Bar-B-Que. Horse isn't on the menu, but if you order the chipped beef sandwich, you won't be disappointed. I used to do their advertising."

We drank iced tea and talked—that is, I talked and she listened. Judy was such an intense and enthusiastic listener, I got the feeling I was being interviewed more than engaged in conversation. She had a reporter's nose for the gentle probe, the hang-in-the-air question, the word prompt. It took me twenty minutes to figure out that as honest as her interest seemed, it was also a devise to guide the conversation away from herself.

"You know, just for the record, I'm supposed to be the reporter around here. Much as I love running off at the mouth about myself, learning a couple of things about you would be fun, and I'm guessing, a hell of a lot more interesting. Do you play the violin? Shoot skeet? Dance the tango?"

"I can't help it, Jack. You're so fascinating. So you're one of those Creeks we keep hoping don't rise?" She dropped her eyes to her hands that were strangling a straw.

"I'm sorry. I've spent my whole life dodging reporters, and now maybe I'm on the brink of dating one. God said 'ha'. Okay, here goes—no, the flute; no; yes. There, that wasn't so hard, I guess. Now let's get back to you." She raised her eyes and got that quiet man stare I learned from Daddy, which broke her precisely as it had broken me all my life.

We sat in silence for a very long ten seconds. "Jack, you just don't know what it's like to be the child of a famous politician, especially one like Lightning Rod Wickerman. You're invisible at first, which is okay, but then I found myself being branded as a sycophant whenever I agreed with my father or a traitor whenever I didn't. I tried for a while to be unobtrusive, but that's just not my nature. This is our time, Jack; this is our century. We need to make the most of it. After this November, things will never be the same.

"I could tell you a thousand things about my past—how I lived at boarding schools since I was twelve; how my mother had just a little bit of the front part of her brain scrambled like an egg to exorcise her demons; how my father pulled strings to get me into Princeton, then cut off my funding two years later when I became a summer intern for Robert Kennedy, who he considered a turncoat. But what good would it do either of us, Jack Harjo? I find my father one of the most repugnant men in America, but if I spend even one day engaging him in battle, he's won. I'm Judy Wickerman, child of the future."

"So that's why you're here, and living at Miss Hetty's? Because the congressman cut you off?"

"Without a cent. Frankly, I'm grateful. I love Oklahoma. I spent the first twelve years of my life and most summers here, and you know something else? This is where it's happening, Jack. Nobody back east seems to know it, but the first successful civil rights demonstration in the country happened right here in Oklahoma City. Clara Luper and twelve of her students from Dunjee High School sat in at Katz Drug Store. You know what she said? 'Thirteen Cokes, please.' That's all. Not another word. And they threw them all in the clink. 'Thirteen Cokes, please.' Isn't that perfect? That's Mahatma on the prairie. Two weeks and two sit-ins later, Katz gave up and not only agreed to serve Negroes at the Oklahoma City lunch counter, but they opened up all their lunch counters in more than thirty drug stores across the Midwest. That's another reason why

I'm back here. I want to get involved in civil rights, and why drive to Mississippi when a black man still can't sit down for a hamburger on Campus Corner. God, I'd love to meet Clara Luper."

"Well, I can help you there," I said and impulsively took her alabaster hand in mine. "Clara Luper is going to be speaking at the All Faiths Center next Sunday afternoon. The *Oklahoma Daily* has assigned me to interview her. Want to come along?"

Judy and the soft-spoken, bespectacled Miss Luper hit it off immediately. In their first meeting, Judy actually became the interviewer and I became the scribe. They agreed to meet again the following week in Oklahoma City, and Judy offered to open some doors for Luper and her students if they wanted to come to Washington.

Then about a month later, I was again playing records on the Radio Free Pizza Hour when the phone rang.

"Radio Free Pizza."

"Will you accept a long distance collect call from Judy Wickerman?" the operator asked.

"Absolutely."

"Hi, Jack. Thanks for accepting my call. I can't talk long. Let the girls at Miss Hetty's know I'm okay, will you. Guess what? I'm with Miss Luper in Tulsa. We just sat in at John A. Brown's and got thrown in jail. Isn't that marvelous?"

CHAPTER 9

To the disappointment of fire-breathers like Zelda and Judy, growing up I never really felt any prejudice against me for being Indian. They wanted me to be angry; they were angry for me. But I just couldn't work up much of a lather. Maybe it was because I'm mixed-blood and my nearly-famous mother was white. I never thought of myself as Indian or not Indian, just Oklahoman, I guess.

But just because I didn't feel prejudice didn't mean it wasn't there. I was just too self-centered to see it. The full-blood kids who went to Carter Seminary, that's the Indian school a few miles north of Ardmore, were so completely shut off from town that they might as well have been going to school on Mars. If we thought of them at all, we considered them stand-offish. The fact that most of them didn't speak English very well was just evidence to us that they were dumb as well as stuck up.

And colored people? I'd play baseball against some of the colored kids from Douglass and Dunbar, and knew the names of most of the best players, but I never saw them off the diamond. Colored people in Ardmore lived in—I can't believe I'm writing this—Nigger Town. And it was a separate world. When coloreds weren't allowed into our lives, they pretended not to care and built a world of their own. Not just schools and ball teams, either. There was the colored picture show where they showed all those colored cowboy movies (they even had their own singing cowboy, Herbert Jeffery, the Bronze Buckaroo), their own newspaper, the Sentinel, and their own radio station, KLVN (all the kids in high school would listen to KLVN late at night because it was the only place you could hear the "dirty bop" songs by Hank Ballard and the Midnighters, Preacher Smith, Clyde McPhatter, Screamin' Jay Hawkins and the Crows. Oh man—"Work with Me, Annie," "Sexy Ways," "Honeydripper," "I Put a Spell on You," "Don't Do It—I Done Done It").

But colored people were only pretending to go their own way. They weren't a bunch of Marcus Garveys; it just suited the white people to think so. Even though I was still in grade school, I remember Old Bob writing an editorial about how at the University of Oklahoma, they did a little pretending of their own. When the US Supreme Court forced OU to admit a black man, George McLaurin, the college roped off a section of a classroom just for him, and made him sit at a separate table in both the library and cafeteria. This "separate but equal" nonsense was crazy, of course, so crazy that the McLaurin decision was used four years later as the basis for Brown V. Board of Education, which ended segregation in American schools in 1954.

But segregation didn't end in restaurants, hotels, barber shops or dentist offices; and once you saw it, really saw it, it looked like a world designed by Lewis Carroll for the Red Queen.

Clara Luper opened my eyes. Although Judy had abandoned her for more confrontational and dangerous civil rights demonstrations in Mississippi and Alabama, I spent a lot of time with the quiet and almost stately Miss Luper that summer. I wrote three pieces about her for the *Ardmorite* that Art Triester, who had moved up to editor, put on page three above the fold, a good spot.

Clara Luper and I drove around a lot of towns in Oklahoma that I had often visited, but not really seen. She showed me a water fountain in a park in Duncan with two bubblers, one marked "Whites Only," the other "Colored." The "Colored" one was broken and rusted. There were white and colored men's rooms at a football stadium in Oklahoma City. That was better than Okemah, where the men's room said "whites only." Colored people in Okemah had to hold it until they got home, which included the colored people who worked there. We were told at a barbeque joint in Wewoka that we'd have to take our food outside, even though it was raining. We visited a dentist's office in Durant with two doors, one marked "whites," the other "colored." The two doors opened into the same waiting room. Lewis Carroll laughed.

One day we sat down at the counter of a coffee shop in the John A. Brown's department store in Tulsa. Only weeks before, Mrs. John A. Brown herself had met with Miss Luper and after a few hours of quiet conversation, announced to the press that forevermore all Brown's coffee shops and tea rooms would be open to everybody, regardless of race or color. It was a proud moment for Miss Luper and I think she wanted to share it with me.

We sat on the red leather swivel chairs of the luncheonette and ordered hamburgers from the waitress in her highly starched brown-and-white-checked uniform. The woman wrote everything down on her pad as if she had been doing it all her life, smiled and scurried back to the kitchen to place her order.

"Well, that was easy," I said. "I don't know what I was expecting, but I sure wasn't expecting anything so, I don't know, run of the mill."

"Yes, Jack Harjo (she always called me by both my names), the walls of segregation can come tumbling down, but first you've got to behold the wall." She looked down at her gloved hands folded in her lap, then looked back at me. "Do you know what freedom is? Freedom is sitting here with you, waiting for a hamburger, and knowing it will come to both of us the same. Victories are no less sweet because they are small."

I was moved beyond anything I had felt before, and when I got back to Norman I wrote an editorial for the university newspaper, *The Oklahoma Daily*, about the experience and my conversations with Miss Luper. The editorial was called "Waiting for a Hamburger" and ended like this: "Sadly if Clara Luper had wanted to enjoy her hamburger on Campus Corner, she'd be waiting still—standing outside, in the back. How long should Clara Luper wait for a hamburger at the University of Oklahoma?"

Normally the lifespan of an editorial, especially one in a college newspaper, can be measured in hours. And so it was with "Waiting for a Hamburger." But this was 1960, the dawn of the tumultuous (word number 89) civil rights era in America, and the press, at least, was fascinated.

My faculty advisor, Mr. Whitaker, who was also publisher of the *Oklahoma Daily*, waved me into his office a few days later.

"Congratulation again on your editorial, Jack, and guess what? *US News and World Report* is going to reprint it in their back-to-school issue in two weeks. They're going to make it the lead in a new feature they're calling "Voices From Campus." You're going to get a hundred bucks out of it, and I got a feeling, a hell of a lot more. That little pebble you threw into the pond may look like a tidal wave by the time it gets to shore. Fasten your seat belt."

He was right, primarily due to my Agitator-in-Chief Judy Wickerman. The night after "Waiting for a Hamburger" came out in the magazine, General Tom and I got a call during the "Radio Free Pizza Hour."

"Hello, this is Radio Free Pizza," I said. "You're on the air."

"Will you accept a long-distance collect call from Judy Wickerman?"

I shot a puzzled look at General Tom, who was paying the phone bill. He nodded.

"Of course." I waited a few seconds and heard a click. "Hi, Judy. Thanks for calling. Where are you?"

"I'm in Birmingham, Alabama, Jack, and everybody's talking about your wonderful opinion piece in *US News and World Report.* You've expressed exactly what all of us down here feel. Look, I don't have a lot of time, but I have a question for General Tom. General, there's no time like the present. Will you pledge right now to be the first eating establishment on Campus Corner to agree to serve people of all races, creeds and colors?"

Tom, who had been sleeping with Zelda the last few months, was ready. "You know, I've been thinking about that, Miss Wickerman, and the answer is absolutely yes. I'll go you one better. To celebrate this long over-due victory, we are going to be sending Radio Free No-Waiting Hamburger Pizza all next week to the men of Alpha Phi Alpha fraternity. That sound all right to you?"

"It would sound better if you included Alpha Kappa Alpha. You got something against women?" There was laughter in the background.

"How about every black Greek house on campus, Miss Wickerman? My apologies. Say, what's all that noise I hear behind you? You at a party?"

"Something like that, General. We're in the Birmingham jail. This was my one phone call. Thanks again. Gotta go."

* * *

I borrowed Leroy's Plymouth, stopped off at Daddy's to get plenty of money for bail and got to Birmingham two days later. Judy was reluctant to come with me at first for fear that she was breaking faith with her sisters, but one woman, obviously the leader, said it was okay; the NAACP was coming to spring them all later that afternoon.

We drove to a Holiday Inn that refused to give us a room because we didn't have any luggage. It probably didn't help that Judy called the manager a fascist.

When we got back in the car, Judy rolled down the window. "Whooee. Sorry, Jack, but a gal can get pretty ripe after three days in the slammer. Tell you what—if a true-blue, anti-communist, freedom-loving coed can't get a shower and a room in Red Neck City without a wedding ring, let's go to New Orleans. I know a great hotel in the French Quarter that doesn't care if you're married, cross-eyed or green. What do you say? Think you can stand the fragrance for a few more hours? When we get there, well, I'm not proposing, but I do propose that we go through a couple of rigorous wedding night dress rehearsals. If we're going to be living together next year, and I've decided that we should, and not at that terrible Los Dones either, then I can't think of a better place to whet our sexual appetites than New Orleans. Hello? Calling Jack Harjo. Did you hear me?"

"I don't think you smell so bad," I said with the heart of a natural-born poet.

CHAPTER 10

With General Tom's help, we set about integrating Campus Corner. Rickner's, which was a book store and cafeteria, agreed quickly, although Zelda said their chili made it a Pyrrhic victory (word number 63). There was a lot of foot-dragging in other spots, however. Even though that was the year that America seemed to discover civil rights, integration didn't go smoothly. Old alliances were broken; new battle lines were drawn.

For starters, my friend Clara Luper refused to have anything to do with it. "I'm sorry, Jack, but this is all getting out of hand. It's just a three-ring circus nowadays," she said, showing her irritation. "When those men from CORE asked me to march with them in Memphis, the leader said we had to wait until the television station got its truck there. And half the marchers seemed to be from some New York college or someplace where they haven't invented soap yet. You all go on and good luck, but I say if you have to wait for the television, I don't know what-all. You're just asking for it."

And of course we were. With the clean successes at Katz Drugs and John A. Brown's, most of the students were lulled into thinking that the integration of restaurants around a university would be a snap. So did the television news people who enjoyed the fact that they weren't getting slapped in jail or whacked in the head by an over-enthusiastic Mississippi policeman. They also loved filming attractive coeds staging "burger boycotts" and singing protest songs.

The hands-down leader of the protest singing was my now ex-roommate Leroy Goss. He had discovered what for him was the best of all worlds—he could hang around campus all day, not really have to go to any classes, sing and play his guitar and get laid on a regular basis. "The poontang's just incredible, Jack," Leroy gushed. "We're talking sorority girls, and not just from here either. Last week I slept with a gal from UCLA who told me she used to be on 'Dobie Gillis.' Chabbabas out to here."

Most of the protest singing and poster-waving took place on the corner by Rickner's. This was directly across from the Georgian-columned Alumni House, so the television cameras could set up an establishment shot. There was just enough honking of horns, cat-calls and cowboys giving the finger from pickups to satisfy the TV folks and put a patina of risk over the brave Thetas and Tri-Delts who were bent on changing the world one hamburger joint at a time.

The patina got a hell of a lot thicker when Leroy, his amp and the Singing Sorority Sisters moved to the other end of the block in front of the Town Tavern. For one thing, the Town Tavern really was a tavern, and it sold beer, pitchers and pitchers of beer to the football-loving rowdies who were only vaguely aware the university was across the street. They came to drink beer and eat pickled hard boiled eggs and talk football. But mostly to drink beer. Oklahoma beer is notoriously weak, but drink enough of it and some guys start feeling like Rocky Marciano, or invisible, or both.

Boycotting the Town Tavern didn't exactly send a chill up the spine of the owners, because the sororities had declared it off-limits for decades. It was a roughneck island in a sea of students, and much to the delight of the camera crews, became the fulcrum (number 22) for confrontation. While the coeds sang "We Shall Not Be Moved," some of the good old boys took to standing in front of the tavern's big plate glass window, waving their pitchers like extras in "The Student Prince," and serenading with songs like "High Above a Pi Phi's Garter," and filthy verses to "These Little Things Remind Me of You." With so much kindling, someone was bound to strike a match.

The scene I'm about to describe next is absolutely true down to the smallest detail. For one thing, I know because Larry Reznick was standing right there among the Cowboy Serenaders when it happened (I always suspected it was Larry who taught them the off-color frat-boy songs that you seldom heard in honky-tonks). For another, every second was caught on film by a crew from WKY-TV.

It was late one Indian summer Saturday afternoon in early October. The Sooners were playing an away game and beating the shit out of Kansas State as usual. It was a slow news day in Oklahoma City, so somebody from the television station (nobody ever admitted who) called Zelda and asked if there was going to be a protest on Campus Corner that afternoon. "Could be," she said. "Let me make a few phone calls."

So Leroy and a dozen of the regulars, bored and restless, set up shop in front of the Town Tavern. Leroy liked his football as much as the next guy, but it was already the fourth quarter and Oklahoma was ahead 42-0, so he plugged in his guitar and gave it a rip. What he hadn't taken into account was the beered-up Town Tavern sports fans listening to the game on the radio, pounding their pitchers on the tables and screaming for blood. If there was anything those guys liked better than a Sooner win it was a Sooner rout. Larry said they were chanting "Hang a half a hundred on 'em," and "Kansas, bloody-nose Kansas."

Larry said that Leroy's amped guitar really was incredibly loud, so nobody's hands were totally clean. The game was just about over and Leroy was singing "We Shall Overcome," at the top of his lungs when all hell broke loose. A few guys sitting closest to the door and therefore, music, grabbed their beers and poured onto the sidewalk. On the film you can hear somebody shout "Hey get a load of that gal from National Geographic." "Fuck you," Leroy suggested. Then a big guy wearing one of those green John Deere baseball caps came flying out of the pack yelling, "Overcome this, mother fucker," and threw his beer bottle at Leroy. It hit Leroy a glancing blow on the shoulder, bounced off and then hit Mari Branson on the forehead, opening a gash that sent blood streaming down her face.

Leroy, who had spun out of the way to deflect the bottle, just kept spinning and came up with the neck of his guitar in both hands, whistling it through the air like a sling blade. He caught the surprised and stumbling man with an upper cut square on the bridge of his nose, dropping him like a Georgia pine. It was such a pure comedic movie moment that a lot of the by-standers started laughing and clapping. But the laughter died down when they saw the blood pooling under the face-down man's head. "He's not moving." the cameraman said.

He never moved again. He was pronounced dead on the way to Norman Muni Hospital. Leroy actually rode in the ambulance with the dead man, muttering "I'm sorry, I'm sorry, I'm sorry, man."

The judge was very sympathetic, but all the prosecution had to do was show the film footage and Leroy was convicted. The judge gave him one year for involuntary manslaughter at McAlester state prison. Leroy did nine months, got off with good behavior and disappeared back into the oil fields. I heard he was up around Borger, Texas, but I never saw him again.

* * *

While I've got jurisprudence on my mind, I might as well tell you about what happened to Larry Reznick, who, unlike Leroy Goss, kept popping up in my life so often I wouldn't be surprised if he's not out there in the hen house right now, plotting my next disaster.

It was Thanksgiving week-end and Judy had gone back to Washington to spend some time with her father and try to patch things up a little. John Kennedy had just been elected president and Judy had been a tireless and outspoken worker for the Kennedy/Johnson ticket. But she had promised the congressman that even though she probably couldn't find it in her heart to vote for him, she wouldn't work for his opponent.

It was an uneasy truce at best, but true to form Arthur Wickerman used it to his full advantage. Kennedy had edged the country ever so slightly to the Democratic side of the aisle, but in typical fashion Oklahoma marched resolutely in the opposite direction, with Wickerman as drum major. He won in a landslide.

The day after his re-election Judy and I watched as he was interviewed by one of the television stations in Oklahoma City. After about three minutes of Wickerman's preening and gloating, the exasperated interviewer decided to take him down a peg.

"But isn't it true, Congressman, that your own daughter was a volunteer worker for Jack Kennedy?"

"Yes, that's true. She and a lot of other young people got caught up in the handsome Bostonian's lofty rhetoric. I admire her youthful exuberance. But believe me when I tell you that my daughter is a firm supporter of me and my desire to see this country free and safe from outside influences."

The reporter's eyebrows went up and, disappointed that she hadn't baited the bear, tried again. "Well, Mister Wickerman, stories coming out of the Kennedy campaign staff give little evidence of that support."

"Absence of evidence is not evidence of absence," Wickerman crooned, and I swear he was looking right at me. I wanted to strangle the television set.

Judy and I had gotten an apartment a few blocks off campus in a leafy faculty section. We'd gotten our own phone and, with Daddy's help, I bought a 1957 gray Ford Fairlane. "As often as your girl friend gets thrown in the clink, Jack, you'd best have a car to spring her," Daddy said with a pat on my back.

So just after midnight Thanksgiving, the phone rang. Judy was a night owl and it wasn't unusual for her to call me this late. In fact I was still up reading a book, trying to come down from the Radio Free Pizza show.

"Radio Free Harjo," I said jauntily. "Hi hon. Please don't tell me you've been thrown in the hoosegow again."

"Hi darling," Larry answered. "Wrong person, right idea. Jack, I'm in jail and I'm not going to shit you, I'm in a world of hurt. I'm in the county jail in Denton and you need to come post bail."

"Are you okay? And what the hell are you doing in Denton, Texas, on Thanksgiving?"

"Yeah, I'm fine. They got me down here for buying marijuana. Now listen. Go to my apartment, wake up Tiger, he's got a key. There's a cigar box in the drawer under my typewriter. Bring it with you. There's at least five thousand bucks in there, and I've got a feeling I'm going to need every penny."

"You got busted for buying grass? I know Texas is a tough state, but five thousand dollars? How much did you buy?"

The voice on the other end got a little shaky. "It was a set up, Jack. The farmer and the sheriff are cousins or something. The farmer sells me the shit, calls his cousin, he nabs me, and they do it all over again the next week." I could hear him cup his hand over the receiver and call to someone in another room. "Yes, sir, I'm coming. Just finishing up." His voice was now a husky whisper. "Don't fail me buddy. I know a lot about marijuana laws down here. If I'm convicted, I could be looking at twenty-five to life. See you in the morning. Please?"

I took off at the crack of dawn and got there just before noon. The bail was set at $2,500, which I paid in cash under the very suspicious eyes of the bailiff.

We got in the car and it was then I noticed the steely look in Larry's eyes. I thought it was just sleep deprivation until he started talking in a flat tone I didn't recognize.

"It's not fair, you know, Jack," Larry said. "Leroy kills a man and gets a year; I buy some grass and will do ten years minimum. Pull over here. I got something to show you."

I stopped in front of an old warehouse. "That's only if you're convicted, Larry. C'mon, we can beat this. Judy knows some first-rate lawyers who'll go to bat for you. What do you want to show me?"

"Look, I'm guilty, okay? They did it perfectly. They got me with five kilos in the trunk. I can't do the time, Jack. Take me to the Greyhound station."

"You don't need to take a bus, Larry. You can't just run away. Where would you go?"

Larry slowly pulled a blackjack out of his aviator jacket. "I bought this off another prisoner last night. Cost me a hundred dollars. Actually I'm not taking the bus, Jack. You are. And if you're thinking I won't hit a friend in the head with this sapper and maybe kill him like Leroy did, you're right. But I'm desperate. I *will* take out your kneecap. I'll break your leg again; the same one you told me you broke in high school. Want to spend three more months in a cast? When I get to Mexico I'll wire Zelda instructions on where you can come to pick up the car." He flashed a smile. "Sorry, old buddy. Thanks for posting my bail and thanks for the loan of the car. I'll make it up to you. I promise."

That was one promise I'm kind of sorry he kept.

CHAPTER 11

Sure enough about a week later Zelda got an envelope with one of those locker keys in it, along with an unsigned note saying the car keys were at the Guadalajara bus station and directions on where to find the car. I asked Judy if she would drive down there with me, but she said she'd just as soon not and besides, she couldn't because she was on her way to New Orleans for a march. Don't worry, she said, the sex will be even better when you get back.

I got a tourist visa and flew to Mexico, my first time in an airplane, and found the car in a parking lot just a block off that plaza where the mariachis are. The car was clean, full of gas and there was even an envelope with two hundred dollars in the glove compartment. Larry is a creep, but an ethical one in his own way.

As much as I liked the prospect of an enhanced version of getting laid, I wasn't nuts about Judy going down south again, even if it was the more cosmopolitan city of New Orleans. I was afraid she'd get her brains bashed in or worse. We'd both seen newsreels of cops in Alabama and Mississippi attacking marchers with fire hoses and German shepherds, and I knew those good old boys played for keeps. Of course, the whiff of danger was just what Judy was after. She thought confrontation was victory. Judy was like a martyr running toward the stake carrying a rope and a box of matches.

I remember seeing a movie when I was eight or nine, one of those black-and-white film noir things that were second features at the drive-in. The star, Steve Brody or somebody, had this awful disease that was creeping up his leg, turning him into stone little by little. Every day he'd mark the progress of the disease by sticking a long pin into his leg right at the point where he could still feel something. Every day he'd move the needle a little farther up his leg. Scared the shit out of me.

I think Judy was afraid she had some disease, too—arthurwickermanitis. She only had to look at her father to see a soul turned to stone, and she wondered if it was genetic. She'd clinically and methodically stick herself with spiritual pins—a lunch counter sit-in over here, three days in a Montgomery jail over there—to probe the disease's progression.

Judy was a danger addict, but she wasn't suicidal; although I remember her telling me she once considered "self-euthanasia." She always said things like that with a laugh, and I thought she was being urbane and witty. But the truth of the matter was Judy didn't like herself very much and spent the entire time I knew her putting herself in harm's way. Over the months we were together in Norman, I appointed myself as her protector as well as lover, although it was the protection provided the damsel by the dragon—clumsy and unwanted.

When I got back across the border, I called Judy and told her I'd like to come along with her to New Orleans. She hesitated just a beat, then said well sure, but we might get tossed into the pokey. I could tell by her voice that she hoped so. She tried to sound serious, but I could hear the little girl enthusiasm hiding behind her words. She said meet her at Tulane, that would be the staging area for the march.

I got a hotel room at The Pontchartrain, just a few blocks up St. Charles Street from Tulane, which Judy refused to stay in because it would break her solidarity with the other marchers. So we both bowed our necks, had our first fight and then, just like she predicted, had the best sex of our lives at the Motel LaSalle over on Magazine. I kept one eye on the door to our room, however. I was kind of afraid the cops would break in and shoot me for raping a white woman. Weird, huh? I never thought of myself as being Indian, but I am kind of dark, and that didn't work. Not down there. I didn't mention this to Judy, of course, but did steer it so she'd be on top, not the usual position for a woman being raped.

I needn't have worried, because all the New Orleans cops must have been out going to Dale Carnegie courses or something. They were nowhere to be seen, and the next morning police lined up politely along the march route, passing out cups of water and oranges to anybody who wanted them. The Reverend Abernathy had told us the night before that passive resistance would be the watchword, and when the police came to arrest us we should simply go limp like a sack of potatoes and go with the flow. I swear there must have been undercover cops at that meeting, because the next day there was no flow. I'd seen Shriners' parades with more action.

We marched, hundreds, maybe thousands of us up St. Charles with Reverend Abernathy, James Farmer and that chipped-tooth folk singer Joan Baez in the lead. We sang all the way to the courthouse, made a few speeches and then everything just sort of petered out. Judy kept cutting her eyes at me like "Is this all there is?" and I thanked God Zelda had stayed in Norman.

I could tell Judy was disappointed. She wasn't going to get a chance to move the pin up her soul.

I had kept the room at the Pontchartrain just in case, and when we got back there, the very unfulfilled Judy Wickerman took out her frustration and hunger on me with an acrobatic fucking. I had known for a long time that making love was an end-game for me, but for Judy it was just a way to feed the beast. Whenever I had a climax, she'd shout triumphantly "That right; that's right. Give it to me. Give it to me." I called it the mating cry of the alpha female. It became a standing inside joke.

Later as we were lying in bed, I lazily drew diagrams on her incredibly white nude body. "You ever see any alabaster?" I asked her, my finger tracing circles around a nipple that was lighter than I was all over.

"Sure. Well, I think sure, in museums and castles and stuff, although I'm not certain I could pick alabaster out of a marble line-up. Why?"

"Because I was going to say you have alabaster skin and it dawned on me I'm not sure what it looks like. Sometimes I use words just because I read them somewhere. Probably some guy in a trashy novel said his girlfriend had skin like alabaster and I filed it away for later use. You won't let me sound like a trashy novel, will you?"

Judy gave that tinny, high-pitched laugh that was a shade too loud and maybe a little contrived. "Too late, my darling buckaroo. But I love every minute of it. What do you want to do tonight? And please don't say Bourbon Street. Barf."

I rolled off the bed and stood in my best Naked Indian pose—strong, but not menacing, I thought. "No, I was thinking somewhere closer to home. Thanks to you, I've gone as nuts over Jack Kennedy as you are. How would you like to go hear Sargent Shriver tonight? He's speaking at Tulane."

* * *

Tulane University looks so much like the mind's eye version of what a university should look like that other universities come to copy it. Live oaks and Spanish moss, ivy walls and little benches set along paths that lead to parks and millionaire mansions, the rickety-rackety wooden streetcars (yes, there's one called Desire. I looked) come together as college heaven. You half expect to see Ronald Coleman, pipe and patched elbows in place, come strolling out of the president's office.

Tulane is more than a university. It's an academic hive. Looking out onto St. Charles, Tulane has Loyola on its left flank and good old Glenda's alma mater Sophie Newcomb on its right. The place is crawling with students.

The night we were there the weather was perfect. It was one of those New Orleans December evenings that don't make sense to anybody from out of town—balmy with that sexy mossy-fish smell coming off the river—but the locals know it's just God's way of saying he's sorry about August.

Judy and I were delighted to be swept up in the mingling mass of student, many of whom had marched with us earlier. Everybody was young, educated, restless and ready for the baton to be passed to us.

And that's just what Sargent Shriver did.

McAlister Hall was overflowing and noisy when he strode onto the stage. The university had provided a lectern for him, but he refused to us it, a gesture my mother and I used to think signaled self-confidence.

Sargent Shriver quickly proved he had much to be confident about. He was handsome, not movie star handsome maybe, but Back Bay banker handsome, the kind of guy you'd want investing your grandmother's trust fund. He had the New England twang that Kennedy only hinted at, and somehow it sounded just right. When he raised his hand in greeting, the auditorium fell quiet.

"Well," he said, "This is the single largest gathering of happy Catholics I've seen since my brother-in-law got elected last month. [laughter] And although you'll never hear it from him, I have it on good authority that while Jack Kennedy will soon be the president for all Americans, we Catholics are going to enjoy most-favored nation status at long last." [wild applause]

Shriver told funny and insightful stories about the campaign tour, months on and off buses, the pancake breakfasts, the barbecues, the dirty-diapered sons and daughters of voters ("A couple of times they smelled so bad we didn't know if Mommy was holding her baby up to be kissed or offering him for adoption."), clog dancing, square dancing and dancing the *hora* ("Here's a secret: Ginger Rogers stepped on his foot. She had to vote for him then.").

Then he got down to the heart of his speech. "Maybe one of the most amazing moments of the whole campaign came two days before the election at the University of Michigan. Speaking without notes, President-elect Kennedy outlined a new international venture that will transform the way young men and women like yourselves will bring democracy and freedom to every corner of this planet. Honestly, to this day we still haven't arrived at a name for this venture, but I can tell you that as of last week, I have agreed to head it up. You know Thanksgiving dinners can get mighty long for nay-sayers at the Kennedy compound.

"Of course, I would never have said no. The incredible enthusiasm those University of Michigan students demonstrated that rainy night has echoed through student gatherings in Indiana, Ohio State, Duke and now to this packed house here in New Orleans.

"John F. Kennedy will soon become the first President of the United States born in this century. And make no mistake, thanks to you this is the American Century. This is a youthful, bold new president with bold new ideas. And his boldest is the one I'm going to present to you tonight.

"Many of you remember those words written by the physician Luke in the scriptures: 'For unto whomsoever much is given, of him shall be much required; and to whom men have committed much, of him they will ask the more.'

"I'm about to ask the more of you. Every president, it seems, fields an army. And so shall President Kennedy [groans]. But this will be an army, not of war, but an army of peace and understanding. After many conversations with world leaders in Ghana, India, Peru and Ethiopia, among others, we have been asked to send, what shall we call them? peace brigades into schools, health centers and villages, working directly with the people to improve the human condition for all in the developing world. This will be a volunteer army of our finest and most motivated young American men and women, diplomats to the world. It won't be easy; if it were easy anybody could do it. It will take a two-year commitment on your part; two years of sleeping on cots perhaps, drinking from mountain streams, eating what the people eat, wearing what the people wear. It will be the hardest job you ever loved. The world is calling. Are you prepared to answer?"

There was a two-second delay while we climbed out of our near-hypnotic state, then the auditorium went wild. Those who weren't standing and clapping were rushing the stage like teen-agers at an Elvis concert. As he would do so many times in the future, Shriver had hit the perfect tone. We were shaking hands and clapping the backs of perfect strangers. Somehow we knew this was our moment.

I turned and grinned at Judy, whose eyes were wide and damp. "What do you think?" I asked over the din.

"That's right, that's right. Give it to me," she laughed, holding my shoulders in both hands.

A little over a year later, after a battery of tests and interviews, Judy and I were among the first volunteers to be selected for what became known as the Peace Corps.

Well, I thought, thanks to the bum leg maybe not a Navy Cross or Silver Star, but two years saving babies in the jungle like Tom Dooley will look good on the resume. The script of "Oklahoma's First Creek Senator" was still in play. But my life just continued to write its own script and drag me along behind it. Judy's screenplay got rewritten, too.

CHAPTER 12

Casimiro stepped on one of my chickens this morning.

It was like a hound dog flushing a covey of quail, all feathers and screams, with the chickens doing that running, hopping, flying death dance. (True to form, chickens are not only the dumbest animals in the world; they can't fly worth a shit, either. But they sure can make noise.)

It was lucky I was already up and going through my morning rituals, or I might have shot the poor old soul. I'm about as jumpy as the chickens anymore, I must admit. But with my less-than-distinguished history as the only ROTC cadet to never fire his rifle, I probably would have missed in any case.

Casimiro was just a puddle of apologies. "I am shameless, don Shack (that's about as close as most Spanish-speakers ever came to pronouncing my name). I was not thinking of you, as I often do, and with great respect. I was thinking only of a saw, which disgraces me. I am sorry unto the heavens."

We walked together to the green tool shed that had been one of the hubs of activity the first time I visited. Every now and then I would pat him on the shoulder in reassurance, marveling once again at the Latino proclivity for linguistic hyper-ventilation.

Together we pulled back the wooden door of the dank, but still tidy tool room of machetes, saws, hammers and a long wooden table with a c-clamp vice at one end. Above the table was a framed photograph that was losing its battle with humidity, but was still surprisingly clear.

Casimiro followed my gaze and became as puffed up and proud as he had been humble only minutes before. "A glorious moment in my life, don Shack. El Che trusted me as no others."

As my eyes grew accustomed to the dark I made out four figures, posing somewhat defiantly for the camera. At the far left was Casimiro, grinning his gap-toothed Dracula smile. Next to him stood Che Guevara with his cigar and, although he was in his thirties, he was sporting what looked like a teen-ager's first attempt at a beard.

Then I actually jerked involuntarily. There staring out at me with a bandoleer of ammo slung over her shoulder and her Medusa nimbus cloud of hair partly covered by a Fidel-style field cap, was Judy.

And next to Judy, taller than the others, with those dark, dangerous eyes and handsome face, was Victor.

* * *

I first met Victor Victorin ("such a winner, they named me twice.") in, of all places, Norman, Oklahoma. Judy and I had been assigned as Peace Corps volunteers in Costa Rica and to our disappointment, found that the Central American Peace Corps training center was the University of Oklahoma. Our trip to exotic lands would begin in my old freshman dorms.

Victor was part of an experiment to train Costa Rican nationals to work side by side with Peace Corps volunteers, and then take over when our tours ended. He seemed an ideal choice. From a wealthy second-generation Argentinean family of coffee growers, Victor spoke nearly-perfect English and had clearly been tapped by somebody in the Costa Rican government to go places. He was a little older than the rest of us. Tall with ancient eyes that gave the illusion that he saw more than we did, he had the quiet authority of a professional athlete and an easy bemused smile that made women want to fuck him and men buy him beers and lend him tools. He accepted them all with equal grace.

He could sing, he could dance the tango, but perhaps his most exotic feature to us young and innocent world-beaters was his claim to know Che Guevara. Not just know him, but go to school with him at the University of Buenos Aires, ride motorcycles together through the Andes and drink Pisco sours. He spun stories of El Che that re-enforced Guevara's mystique and we hung on every word. Especially Judy. Victor Victorin was catnip to Judy.

But I'm getting ahead of my story.

* * *

Judy and I had been unraveling as a couple for some time. Looking back, I think we latched on to the idea of going into the Peace Corps together the way a loveless couple decides to have a baby.

There was never any doubt that Judy would get into the Peace Corps; even her father was enthusiastic, glad to get her out of the country for a few years.

I was still iffy, however, at least in Judy's eyes. "We may have to play up your being Indian a little," she told me one night back in Norman. "The selection process is brutal, and I sure wouldn't want to lose you now," she said with hollow sincerity. I just nodded, feeling dead inside.

She wanted to go to Ethiopia or Ghana or some other African nation where rebels and revolutionaries were hiding behind every tree. I wanted adventure and Africa sounded as good to me as anywhere, but I did mention that Larry had said that the most beautiful country in the world was Costa Rica. "We're not going into the Peace Corps as tourists, Jack," she sighed, "but if it will make you feel better, why don't we put it down as our second choice."

Somewhat to Judy's surprise, I think, we both got letters of acceptance and were assigned to the new Republic of Congo. The charismatic (variation on word number 11) Patrice Lumumba had just been assassinated, and our government was scrambling to make nice with the new guys in power. We were supposed to train at Princeton, Judy's old stomping grounds, but a few months before the training began, there was another civil war in the Congo and the deal was off. So it was to be Costa Rica via the University of Oklahoma, Theta burgers and 3.2 beer.

Judy took me walking along the leafy and squirrel-infused north campus on the warm May morning our relationship committed suicide.

"Jack, as soon as classes are over, I'm moving back to Washington to tie up a few odds and ends before training begins in June. This is a little difficult, and I'm sorry. Please bear with me. You see, I thought we'd be going a thousand miles away, and things like closing the apartment would take care of themselves. I never thought for a second that we'd just be going six blocks south."

"Difficult how?" I asked unnecessarily.

"We're on the threshold of our Great Adventure (I could actually hear the capital letters), our Grand National Experiment. With Kennedy at the helm, this is our generation, our generation on the world stage and I want to take every advantage of it. The only way we could have gone into the Peace Corps with the same arrangement we have now is to get married, and I just can't do that, Jack. Sorry."

"Arrangement? That's what we are to you? An arrangement?" I have no idea why I kept asking these asinine questions. I guess I felt that at least one of us ought to make a show of anger or loss, so I gave her the Poor, Poor Pitiful Me Latent Hostility Overstep I had used so effectively with Glenda.

"Oh, Jack, for goodness sakes. You're the one with the list of words. Pick one. I don't want us to go into the Peace Corps as lovers, but I'd prefer we not go in as enemies. We've had our time together and we've helped each other grow. And we won't grow apart. We'll just be on a higher plane. Can I have your hand on this?"

She actually held out her hand, which surprised me almost as much as the fact that I shook it. By this time my mind was filling with vipers of rejection and I wanted to say something hurtful, but a gust of wind sent her unruly red hair into her eyes, which were staring intently into my soul, looking for absolution. Astonished, I found that love/hate thing that has made fools of so many men stuck in my throat.

"Deal," I said in my best imitation of Sydney Carton going to the guillotine.

CHAPTER 13

I'm not sure what people mean when they say "happy." Old Bob told me never to use the word in reporting. "Say he was smiling or chuckling or doing cartwheels or dancing the Charleston, but don't say happy. You don't know if he's happy or not, and probably he doesn't either. He could be winning the Irish Sweepstakes on the same day he gets his eye poked out."

Okay. Fine. Having said that, June 21, 1962, came as close to being a happy day for me as I'm likely to get on this planet.

It certainly was magical; so magical it made me smile. Smart, good-looking, energetic men and women exactly my age came tumbling out of the trees, buses, trains, balloons and airplanes and landed, plunk, in the dormitories just south of the Oklahoma University campus. Even Judy, who was far more accustomed to impressing than vice versa, couldn't believe her eyes. With their duffle bags and Ipana smiles, these were the cream of the crop, some of the first batches of Peace Corps volunteers. These were the Kennedy Kids, the young denizens of Camelot, hand-picked to spread American values to every corner the world, the more remote the better. Sargent Shriver's words had become a recruiting poster mantra: "The hardest job you'll ever love," and we were head over heels. In a matter of hours, I could sense that this was the group I had always wanted to be measured by. I was finally part of something big.

We sat around the cavernous cafeteria drinking coffee and that orangeade that seems to come uninvited to every summer camp and college campus in America, spinning our bare-bones bios that we would flesh out over the summer.

The force field of confidence in that big hall was so crackling with energy that birds could not have flown through it. They wouldn't have wanted to leave anyway, because the self-introductions were as interesting as they were humorous, occasionally hilarious.

There was Ernie Mason, a cocky graduate of Fordham who showed up wearing lederhosen and carrying a dog-eared copy of "Great Expectations" in Spanish. There was Walt Connolly, a string bean who had played basketball at Marquette and would soon become the tallest man in Costa Rica. Jeannie Carter had spent one summer barnstorming with the Hollywood Redheads women's baseball team and played against Al Kaline in summer league. I had already heard of Collette Johnson, who had written of being the first black student at Southern Methodist University in a series of articles for *Ladies Home Journal.*

When it came Judy's turn, she talked about being an Oklahoma graduate and offered to show us all the sights. She also kept the group enthralled with her stories of sit-ins and Birmingham jails. I noticed, however, there were two things she failed to mention—Arthur Wickerman and me.

When she finished, Ernie Mason held up his hand. "Excuse me, but are you any kin to that Red-baiting Congressman Wickerman?"

Judy didn't miss a beat. "Yes, until I was able to get a quickie divorce in Reno last year, he was my father. There was no alimony involved, but he did get custody of all my Republican friends, both of them." I was grateful for the chance to hide behind the roar of laughter, but it stung a little. So maybe Old Bob was right—happy and not happy.

Finally I stood up and acknowledged that Judy and I were both from Oklahoma and graduates of OU, giving the impression that we barely knew each other, and who would have guessed that we would both be going to Costa Rica and so on and so on until Collette jumped to her feet. "Wait a minute," she shouted, pointing her finger at me. "Finally I made the connection. Jack Harjo? Waiting for a Hamburger Harjo? I've still got that article you wrote for US News in my wallet. Damn, Jack Harjo. Come over here and sit by Collette. We've got some stuff to do."

* * *

We talked deep into the night, moving our talkfest to the large combination living room and library with its dozens of chairs, sofas and card tables. We draped ourselves over couches, sat on coffee tables and stretched out on the floor, loving being young, loving being alive, loving being together.

Finally around midnight a custodian pushing one of those barrels on wheels flicked the lights off and on in the unmistakable gesture to break it up. "Go to bed, go to bed, go to bed," he said with a laugh. "You've got three more months of this, and I can't go home until all these ashtrays are empty."

I recognized the voice. "Tiger?" I shouted and waved. "Tiger Moran? It's me, Jack."

He looked up with that perpetually pleasant but slightly fogged-in expression. "Well, Jack Harjo, I sure didn't expect to see you. Where have you been hiding? What are you doing out here so late at night? Do you know some of these people?"

"Believe it or not, I *am* some of these people, Tiger. I'm in the Peace Corps." I'd gotten alongside him, and dropped my voice. "Judy is here, too, but we're not seeing each other anymore, maybe not even talking, so mum on that one, okay?"

"The redhead? To tell you the truth I'm not so good with names, never have been, so no problems there. It's good to see you, Jack. We've missed you over at Los Dones. I'm going to tell Zelda. She'll go nuts. And believe me she'll be more than happy to help you get over the redhead, if you know what I mean."

Just then I felt a hand on my shoulder. I turned to see the director Tom Vaughn.

"Lights out, fellows." He paused. "Did I hear you call him Tiger?" He paused again. "Holy shit. El Tigre? Chico Moreno? It is you, by God. Chico, remember me? Tommy Hood? I fought you in Guadalajara in, when was it, '47, '48? You hit me so hard you knocked me all the way into college. So you're living in Oklahoma these days? I thought you'd be king of Mexico by now, at least."

"Never could learn the damn lingo," Tiger said amiably. "Tommy Hood, Tommy Hood . . . yeah, I remember you. Tall skinny kid with a good chin. Able to take a punch. How are you, Tommy?"

"It's Tom now, Tiger. And it's lucky I can still take a punch. I'm the Peace Corps director for Latin America these days. Try getting into that ring someday. Look, I've got to hustle. Got to go to Oklahoma City to pick up the Costa Rican guys for this new leadership program we're trying out. I imagine they'll be feeling no pain. That red eye LACSA flight is just an open bar with wings and a propeller. I may need you tomorrow when they sober up. You still play that mean guitar? It speaks Spanish like a dream, as I remember, even if you don't. See you guys tomorrow."

I just stared at Tiger. "Damn, Tiger, you're a true man of mystery. I know you paint and used to box, but the guitar? Why didn't you ever say anything?"

"Aw, Leroy was way better than me, and besides that I can only play in Spanish. See you tomorrow, Jack. I'm the custodian here during the summers."

* * *

Bloodshot didn't begin to describe the eyes of the fourteen men standing uneasily at parade rest in front of us the next afternoon. Although there was no dress code, most of them wore the white short-sleeved shirts and khaki pants we found out later had been issued by the Costa Rican government. They were considerably older than we were, or at least looked older, with their nearly-ubiquitous moustaches and Rudolph Valentino hair. Only Victor Victorin, clean-shaven in a blue button-down shirt and tassel loafers, seemed perfectly at home. He was also by far the most fluent in English.

"Hello, everybody," he said in a buttery baritone. "My name is Victor Victorin, and I'll be introducing my comrades to you a little later. I'm afraid their English isn't much better than the Spanish of many of you, so we've all got a lot of work to do this summer. Let me say we are very glad to be in Oklahoma. Now we can play that famous game of cowboys and Ticos." He laughed musically.

"Oh my God is he cute," whispered Martha Burton, our Alabama cutie.

"And he speaks English better than I do," said Walt Connelly.

Tom Bach, another Marquette grad and our best Spanish-speaker, elbowed Walt gently. "In your case, that's not much of a stretch. But how is he at free throws? And what's a Tico? Is that like a taco, only further south?"

We soon learned that Ticos are what Costa Ricans call themselves, but we learned little else at first from the aloof Costa Rican men. We were together formally only at dinner anyway, and in the beginning only Victor and one of the Juans broke ranks and sat at the English-speaking tables (there were three men named Juan, and to our untrained eyes their mustaches and pompadours made them seem so similar we called them Juan Two Three). I couldn't help but notice that Victor's table was usually lop-sided with women, including, inevitably, Judy Wickerman.

It was Tiger who finally broke the diplomatic ice jam. One night after dinner, he and Tom Vaughn placed themselves strategically in the living room where you virtually had to stumble over them to get to the front door.

Tiger was strumming an acoustic guitar that looked as old and weather-beaten as he did. Tom Vaughn was plucking at something I had never seen before, something that looked like a guitar for giants that I later discovered was called a *guitaron*, and served as a string bass.

"What do you say, Tiger? Remember any of the old songs? How about 'Lupita,' or 'Piel Canela?' 'El Reloj?' 'La Llarona?' I know most of the verses to that one."

True to his word, Tiger's guitar playing sounded very Mexican, with heavy thumbing on the bass strings and rough arpeggios to introduce each verse. He and Tom Vaughn made a good duo, because Vaughn knew the words to every song, or so it seemed, and wasn't afraid to sound off. By the time they had finished "La Llarona" and moved into "Lupita" they had drawn quite a crowd, both American and Costa Rican. Every Costa Rican knew "Lupita," which was as familiar to them as "Let Me Call You Sweetheart" is to us, and just as old. Even a couple of volunteers knew this one, and pretty soon we were all singing along. The only thing missing was a campfire.

The after-dinner hootenanny soon became a regular occurrence. A guy named Claudio had a terrific tenor voice and taught us many of the beautiful Costa Rican songs we would hear in our villages—"Caballito Nicoyano," "Ticas Lindas," "Amor de Temporada," and what turned out to be their national song, "La Guaria Morada."

"Three-chord diplomacy," Walt Connelly called it, and brought his banjo down a few times, but outside of the ranchero songs about getting drunk, it sounded out of place. Of course there were quite a few songs about getting drunk, and not a few of the Costa Ricans were more than willing to practice what they sang.

I noticed that Victor and Judy didn't sing much, but sat together a little back from the rest, Judy leaning into Victor as if by accident at first, sending an unmistakable message to the other women in the group that she was staking her claim. One evening she noticed my questioning gaze and responded with innocent up-turned eyebrows and a one-shoulder shrug that told me everything. I was actually surprised that aside from a twinge of jealousy I felt very little, maybe even a touch of relief.

On Monday nights Dick Chambers, who was a political science major from Harvard, would lead lively discussions about current events, our place in world affairs, and how to spread democracy to other countries. Victor, which of course meant Victor and Judy, never missed these sessions and served as Dick's gadfly.

"How can you justify the embargo of Cuba when only ninety miles from Miami babies and old people are dying from lack of medicine? Do you hate Communism so much you are willing to sacrifice babies on your alter of democracy?" Victor asked, his voice rising.

"I didn't know we were withholding medicine," Judy said. "Can that possibly be true?"

"Whoa, Victor, as much as I respect your views, that's being a bit unfair," said Dick." You know as well as I that Cuba trades with Mexico, cigars and rum out, medicine, clothes and cooking oil in. The embargo is to keep heavy equipment, heavy Soviet equipment, including missile parts, from landing ninety miles offshore. That ninety-mile coin has two sides. Cuba should pick its friends a little more carefully."

Victor rose to his feet. "Cuba didn't choose the Soviet Union. She was driven into Russian arms by your General Eisenhower. And as difficult as life in Communist Cuba may be today with the American embargo, it is one thousand times better than it was under Batista. And Batista didn't care about Cuba; he only cared about Havana and his casinos and his Mafia boyfriends."

"Damn, Victor," Ernie said casually, "All the Cuban Commies I've ever seen in photographs are wearing army fatigues and sporting beards that make them look like they fell off a box of cough drops. You are the first Communist I've ever met in gabardines and loafers. You look like you just walked out of an Esquire magazine."

Victor sat back down and opened his hands in a sign of friendship. "First of all, I'm not a Communist," he said in a voice half an octave lower than before. "And believe it or not, neither is El Che. I've told some of you that I know Che Guevara. We knew each other in college in

Buenos Aires. I am proud to call him friend. You would like him. Fidel's a Communist now; maybe he had no choice. But Che and I are social democrats. Social democracies are the wave of the future. Look at Sweden. Che and I believe that when true socialism is allowed to flourish, people in every country, perhaps even the United States, will embrace it."

"We are on our way to Costa Rica," Tom Bach said. "Do you think Costa Rica should be socialist?"

"Eventually, yes, it will be, and it will be an orderly transition," Victor said. "Don't forget, Costa Rica is already a democracy, and a nation of peace. We don't even have a standing army. But it is not Costa Rica we, and I believe you, should worry about. It is that sad Guatemala, where the generals make whole villages disappear overnight if it pleases them. And it is even sadder Nicaragua, where that devil dictator Somoza strafes *campesinos* in airplanes given him by the US Air Force. When changes come to these countries, as they must, the reaction will be as bloody and oppressive as the regimes they topple. You and I can help them become little Swedens, or they'll become little Cubas. We need your help."

"Well, you've certainly got mine," Judy said defiantly.

John McNaughton learned over and whispered in my ear. "Was she talking about her help or her panties?"

* * *

Three weeks later I had a summer cold and begged off swimming with the rest of the volunteers to catch some shut-eye in my room.

When I got back to the mostly-deserted dorms, I saw Judy loading luggage into the trunk of a limo.

"Hey, Judy, what's going on?" I asked. "Going on a trip?"

She stared at me for a second, and then puffed a sigh of resignation. "Hello, Jack. Well, this is a little awkward. I was kind of hoping to slip out without saying goodbye. But here you are. Yes, I'm leaving, Jack. I've decided Costa Rica doesn't need me and I don't feel like a two-year vacation. I think I can make a much greater impact somewhere else, maybe in Africa like we first talked about. I've asked the Peace Corps to keep me in mind for an assignment in Ghana or Ethiopia. Maybe I can even go to Guatemala and help turn it into Sweden." She laughed hollowly.

I was surprised. "It's not me, is it? Seriously, if you and Victor want to get together, that's between the two of you. I'm a big boy."

"That may be part of it," she said, looking down. "It's complicated. Let's just say goodbye, Jack. Maybe we'll cross paths again someday."

That evening at dinner the cafeteria was buzzing. I barely got my tray on the table when I was peppered with questions.

"Hey, Harjo, did you hear that Judy Wickerman quit?" Walt asked. "You guys were classmates, right?"

"I don't think she quit," I said. "I talked to her a little bit and she said she had asked the Peace Corps to reassign her, maybe to Africa."

"So that's her story, huh?" John McNaughton snorted. "There is an alternate one. Like the one about Tiger catching her and Victor fucking their brains out in the music room behind the piano. I heard Tom Vaughn was furious."

"I don't know why," Walt said in mock innocence. "She and Victor were just playing cowgirls and Ticos. Somebody's got to ride that pony."

CHAPTER 14

With the weight of Judy off my chest, Peace Corps training felt almost like camp to me and in fact became one of the best times of my life. There were a few bumps in the road, of course. Ernie Mason got sent home through the Orwellian process known as deselection; so did a guy named Ralph from Pocatello who nobody knew very well (which was probably the point). We lost two Costa Ricans who took a cab to Pink's Beer Emporium down by the Canadian River, introduced everybody there to *Flor de Caña* rum, got into a brawl and were thrown into the Purcell jail.

Two other Ticos returned home early when I took the group to the Indian Powwow at Anadarko and they wound up, drunk again, at the end of the Pawnee women's line dance in front of the grandstands. That left only Victor, whose brief encounter with Judy had only burnished his reputation, Juan and Two (Three had been in the fight at the river), Claudio the tenor and six others so homesick they rarely left their dorm rooms. It was clear that this was not only the first, but almost certainly the last cross-cultural Peace Corps experiment during Tom Vaughn's tenure.

The rest of us had a blast. We played soccer in the morning before breakfast, a brand of roughhouse soccer unrecognizable to the Ticos. They wanted absolutely nothing to do with us, because our idea of defense was to kick the ball at them as hard as we could and hope for the best. I would remember our reckless abandon later when I became the player/coach/commissioner of the baseball co-op and got plinked on a regular basis.

We studied Spanish from breakfast to lunch, with small classes set to our abilities. Some of the volunteers like Tom Bach were already fluent and simply worked on regional variations. Most of us were sort of in the middle, having taken a course or two in college. And then there were guys like John McNaughton, who made Tiger Moran look like a linguist. Throughout his time in Costa Rica, the big Irishman just couldn't make himself understood. He reckoned this had less to do with his ability to speak the language and more on the probability that most of the nation was hard of hearing. He shouted his mispronounced vocabulary at everybody—cab drivers, school teachers, priests, shoeshine boys—in a volume that could startle horses in the field. But he was so jovial and sincere, people tolerated it as long as they could, all the time looking for a back door.

The poor Peace Corps was caught flat-footed when it came to Spanish instructional material. The American government was used to sending people to foreign consulates, but not orphanages, clinics and one-room schools in the jungle.

The only Spanish books we had were from the Foreign Service Institute, and while it would be unfair to call them useless, they were certainly ripe for criticism. Collette and I even developed a skit made up mostly of real phrases and sentences from the FSI manuals combined with the in-country work many of us knew lay ahead:

"Would you like to play a set of tennis with the orphans, Mister Vice President?"

"Please send to my room two coffees with milk, cookies, a hammer and toilet paper."

"Is that a typical saw? Are they manufactured nearby?"

"Can you direct me to a bathroom?" "Yes, it is 300 paces south of the American Embassy."

I just thought of one last McNaughton/Spanish story: Friday night dinners were "Spanish Only" meals. This cut chatter to a minimum at most tables, but poor John's table was always shrouded in silence. "Pasa me the salt," John said sullenly one night.

"*Solamente Español,*" Martha said brightly as she passed the table.

"Yeah, yeah,' John pouted. "Okay. Pasame la fucking sal, por favor. Better?"

As you might imagine, like my daddy's "smart as I want to be," "Pasame la fucking sal" became standard conversational fare around Peace Corps tables for months to come.

Speaking of Daddy (isn't it time that the raja of ganja and prince of pot start calling his father something a little more grown up?), he came up to visit in early August. With Tom Vaughn's blessing, Daddy took us all out in school buses to the reservation at Little Ax for a powwow and barbeque. He told us all about the Creek traditional corn dances, which marked the Creek new year, and then some of the Little Ax women did a shortened version of the ribbon dance and some men did a hunter's dance. Then we all drank beer. Then we ate chopped beef and blue corn bread. Then we drank some more beer. Then we ate that shitty burnt-hominy *sofki.* Then we drank some more beer. Then we swam half-naked in the Canadian River. Then, wrapped in towels, we smuggled as many beers as we could onto the bus and came home. Great night.

Nobody else in the training program had a car, so I gave mine to Zelda for safekeeping. Just as Tiger had predicted, Zelda was very grateful and would drive over on our free Sunday nights to bring me back to Los Dones for bowls of never-ending stew with Mari and Nigel. Zelda also made various offers to relieve me of tension and stress by conjugal (number 9) visits to her apartment. I don't know how much credit I should get for saying no thank you the first three times. Radio Free Pizza, by the way, had gone off the air when General Tom abruptly sold his place, blew town owing everybody money and opened an up-scale restaurant in Tulsa called Tom Angus' Steak House.

Mostly all the volunteers, including me, never left the south campus confines of the University of Oklahoma. My old landlady at Los Dones, Rosalie Charles, and her family owned a Mexican restaurant called the Monterrey where we would go to practice our Spanish, drink beer and eat enchiladas, which we thought was good training for the food we would encounter later. Little did we know that Costa Ricans considered Mexican food every bit as exotic as we did. When Ticos went out to eat, they ate Chinese or Italian, just like everybody in Peoria.

Our days were full—early morning soccer, then Spanish all morning, then Latin American studies, history, comparative governments, art, music—the whole package. And always the conversations, the table talk, arguments, talk, talk, talk that enriched our lives and made us family.

Family, but not lovers. Although we were mostly young and single, aside from Judy and Victor there was almost no pairing off of volunteers, either that summer or later in country. There were two married couples who entered training, but one of them, the Henleys from Seattle, were swiftly deselected when it was discovered that cute-as-a-button AAU swimming star Anita Henley was only slightly smarter than a button as well. When asked to name the three branches of government, she said the Senate and the House of Representatives but she could never remember the other one. When told she was a little off, she burst into tears and said who needs to know that dumb stuff, anyway. The other couple, the O'Neals, were in their forties and willingly served as our scout masters and surrogate parents. They were high school teachers with no kids of their own, seeking adventure. When we learned that Mrs. O'Neal was originally from Kansas, we immediately started calling her Auntie Em, which made her blush with pleasure.

The rest of us pretty much acted as a unit, a leaderless posse of goodwill. After years of competing to make the team, the right Greek house, the best grades, the best grad school, this was a refreshing respite where leadership was both assumed and meaningless. We all knew that when we got to Costa Rica we would be banished two-by-two from the Peace Corps ark into the jungles and villages where leadership might be misinterpreted as arrogance. We were supposed to blend in, not stand out. So outside of the not-very-real threat of deselection, which John McNaughton called the Nail File of Damocles, we relaxed. We studied together, ate together, sang together, played together. We were indistinguishable; until one day we weren't.

There is a Japanese saying that the exposed nail gets hammered down. How could I have guessed that I would become that nail?

CHAPTER 15

Then one day in late August everybody vanished just as quickly as they had appeared, leaving Tiger and me waving goodbye from the dorm steps like grandpa and grandma waving the kids out of sight.

The night before the exodus, the Peace Corps threw us a big farewell dinner, with Sargent Shriver's number two or three man (I can't remember his name) delivering a mirthless address Walt described as "the seventh-most boring speech of the twentieth century." Then we were told to pack up and meet in two weeks in Miami to fly as a group to San Jose.

I retrieved my car from Zelda and drove to Ardmore where I stored it in Daddy's barn alongside Tafah. Art Triester insisted on writing a front-page story and photo in the *Ardmorite*, one of those "small town boy conquers the universe" stories that I could have written in my sleep. I found it embarrassing and hoped it would soon be forgotten; which it almost was.

Daddy drove me down to Dallas where I boarded the first jet airplane of my life. We spent two incredibly hot and muggy days in Miami that Jeannie Carter said were our final and secret deselection tests before embarking to Ticolandia.

Of course we flew the official Costa Rican airline LACSA, the "open bar with wings," and of course we arrived a little wobbly. We got to the quaint little San Jose airport in a monsoonal downpour, the men wearing white shirts and ties that stuck to our perspiring bodies and the women in dresses, melting straw hats, high heels and white gloves, each of us vowing under our breath never to be seen dead in these outfits when we hit our villages. That proved an easy vow for me to keep, at least—two months later my sports coat and dress shoes were both mildewed and falling to pieces.

San Jose was a beautiful little city, but it smelled funny. We found out later that the smell was from the huge rum factory just across the park from our pension, but to us that first day it just smelled sticky sweet, damp and dangerous.

It also smelled very, very far from home.

The second night at dinner at our pension, I found half a dozen tiny ants floating in my cabbage soup, so I decided to take a walk. John McNaughton caught up with me and gave me a look like his dog had just died.

He shook his head in disbelief. "Holy shit, Jack, I'm a fucking man of the world. How can I possibly be homesick in only 48 hours? Now I know how those poor Costa Ricans felt in Norman. I'm not hungry, are you?"

"Not anymore," I said. "I bagged my limit of ants. I'm trying to cut down on my protein intake. Let's go find a beer."

We went about three blocks, then turned the corner and found a large corner open-air restaurant with bright lights streaming into the park across the street. The place looked very American, with gleaming aluminum-legged tables, even a juke box. Across the front was a large Coke sign that read Bar Soda Palace. Next to it was another sign with the unmistakable curlicue ice cream cone that was as familiar to John and me as Howard Johnson's. We each ordered a cone, ate it like five-year-olds, and then plotted our triumphant return to the pension.

"Hey, everybody, guess what?" John shouted as we burst into the dining room. He could be just as loud and robust in English as Spanish, and twenty pairs of eyes snapped to attention. He roared with laughter. "I'm too excited. You tell 'em, Jack."

I was on to his game, so I just pointed toward the front door and moved my lips, pretending I was too dumbstruck to make a sound. "Dairy Queen," I croaked finally, shaking my finger. "Dairy Queen."

"We're saved," Collette sang and dropped to her knees.

It was actually a Sort of Dairy Queen; not the real McCoy, but close enough. The Bar Soda Palace was run by a guy named Oldimar who had been to Los Angeles a couple of times and was hell-bent on bringing as much of it back to Costa Rica as his entrepreneurial mind could envision. He even served something he called "pie," which drew perplexed stares from the locals, because the word "*pie*" in Spanish means "foot."

Oldimar spoke a fractured and slangy English that was funny and kind of endearing. "Hey you boy from Oklahoma, you give me one cigarette today for please," he said to me one afternoon, and laughed triumphantly at his uncanny command of the language.

Everybody liked Oldimar, his restaurant and his ice cream (which was actually called Los Gigantes because of the two mountains of ice cream logo on the soft-serve machine). We soon discovered that the Bar Soda Palace was where everybody, at least everybody who spoke English, eventually wound up. We also found Oldimar to be a limitless fount of knowledge on just about everything—where to change your money (the street rate was higher than the bank rate), the best buses to the beach and cheap places to stay once you got there, where to buy Playboy magazine (officially outlawed in Catholic Costa Rica), which bars were "family" and which were whorehouses, and which black-market sellers of pre-Columbian art you could trust. The place became a hangout, not just for those of us in the Peace Corps, but sooner or later, almost every American in Costa Rica—including Larry Reznick, but I'm getting ahead of my story as usual.

* * *

The morning before we were scheduled to leave for our villages, we all gathered in the conference room of the rambling second-floor offices of the Peace Corps. Incredibly, many of us still hadn't received our assignments yet, and we were nervous and chatty.

Tom Vaughn, who had made only token appearances since we arrived, stood at the front of the room with a very tall and skinny man in a seersucker suit and bow tie.

"I'm afraid this is sort of a hail and farewell, guys, not just for you, but for me as well," Vaughn said. "The Peace Corps has asked me to return to the United States to train a new group of volunteers coming to El Salvador so, believe it or not, I'm on my way back to the University of

Oklahoma. But you're in luck. I'd like you to meet my friend Frank Le Pommes." He placed his hand on the tall man's shoulder. "Frank's just like you in many ways. When he heard about the Peace Corps, he dropped everything to join. Of course, unlike you he heard about the Peace Corps from his neighbor Sargent Shriver, so it would have been hard to say no. While I'll be hopping from Oklahoma to El Salvador, Frank is taking over as the Peace Corps director for Costa Rica. You're going to like Frank. He was all-American in lacrosse at Harvard, plays the double bassoon and speaks forty-seven languages. Actually I made the bassoon part up. Frank?"

Le Pommes sounded so much like Jack Kennedy we thought he was joking at first. We kept looking back and forth at each other in a mixture of amusement and, frankly, resentment. He was the new kid on the block and we weren't much interested in what he had to say. We weren't hostile, exactly, but we were feeling a little clubbish, and with our natural apprehension about being launched into the unknown the very next day, Le Pommes was dead on arrival. But he tried.

"Alas, Tom, you are also about forty-six languages off the mark. I'm still struggling with English." (He was the first person I'd ever heard use the word "alas" and it sounded just as corny as I thought it would.) "I'll be picking up my Spanish right along with many of you. Is John McNaughton here?"

John waved his fingers at about ear level and glared at the new guy.

Le Pommes laughed heartily. "Well, besides a New England accent, I understand we share a tin ear for the old *Español*. I guess we'll be hitting the *libros* pretty hard, huh?" He laughed again.

John bent over and moved his chair, making a scraping sound on the wooden floor. "Fuck you very much," he muttered under his breath. He straightened up. "Pretty darn hard, you bet, sir," he said brightly.

Tom Vaughn heard both the mutter and insincere response, understood, and stepped in to save the clueless Le Pommes. "Listen everybody, the reason you haven't seen much of me lately is because Frank and I have been going to your towns and villages making sure you have places to stay and food to eat. There aren't Dairy Queens in every town, you know."

There was a nervous titter of laughter that died when we looked into Vaughn's eyes. "Seriously, this is going to be a test for some of you at first. Some of these villages are pretty simple, especially to American eyes. But give them a chance—you'll quickly find that these are the friendliest people in the western hemisphere. You will feel at home in no time. We've tried to pair you up as much as we can, but as you know there are more guys than women, so some of you are going to be on your own. Those of you who are going to isolated villages will be getting a foot locker of books to keep you company."

Vaughn started reading off our assignments. Collette, whose Spanish wasn't much better than John's, got teamed up with fluent Jerry Festa in the pretty Caribbean port town of Limon. Jeannie got a Catholic orphanage in the old city of Cartago; and John was assigned as an English teacher in the former American Fruit Company town of Golfito. "I'm going to have English-only Fridays," John said. "That should give me some peace and quiet."

When it came my turn, Tom Vaughn chuckled conspiratorially. "And the winner of our first foot locker is none other than our very own Sooner, Jack Harjo. Jack, you are on your way to San Isidro, near Lake Nicaragua. You'll be heading up the northern frontier baseball league and working with a farm co-op they're just getting started. It's lucky you're a country boy, Jack. It's beautiful, but a little isolated up there."

"A little isolated?" Frank said in that laugh-talk that I was already growing to despise. "Brother. You're entering two-foot-locker country, Harjo, old man."

CHAPTER 16

For the first time since I'd been in Costa Rica I sat alone at the counter at the Bar Soda Palace, staring at my bowl of near-ice cream. Oldimar was hovering nearby, the smoke from his dangling cigarette squinting his face into a pirate grin.

I liked sitting there and speaking English with Oldimar. He was smart and observant and his English, while adventurous, was pretty good; certainly better than my Spanish. And it made me feel less homesick.

"You lonely, boy from Oklahoma?" he asked with real concern in his voice.

"Not really. Just sort of confused. What's Spanish for "confused?"

"Same thing: *confundado.* When you not remember, think of—what is it?—big old college word and add *ado.* Spanish makes sense, not like your goddam language. Why confused?"

"Well, I've been spending all day long at the bus station waving goodbye to everybody as they got on their buses to their villages. By the way, you've got more damn funny buses down here than I've ever seen. Looks like somebody got drunk and painted a bunch of school buses all crazy-ass colors, then put fringe and shit all over them, and then gave them crazy-ass names like The Angry Horse and The Baby Jesus. Anyway, they're all riding off in rattle-trap stink pot buses. But not me. No sir. I'm being flown into San Isidro on LACSA tomorrow like I'm some sort of big-wig. Why the special treatment, I wonder?"

Oldimar pulled the cigarette from his mouth and used it like a wand. "No special treatment, Oklahoma boy. You fly to San Isidro because there is no road. They think you come to build crazy-ass road so they can ride on crazy-ass buses."

* * *

Any ideas of being a big-wig or getting special treatment vanished the next morning when I got on a dilapidated DC-3 that had to be as old as I was. Most of the seats had been removed to accommodate the incredible amount of sacks of beans and rice, boxes stuffed with all sorts of food and clothing, small parts for machinery, jeroboams (38) of cooking oil, square tin drums of fuel, and vegetables in plastic netting. I saw my foot locker of books peeking out from under a large sack of black beans and some netting filled with soccer balls. Sitting atop the pile was what I took to be a twelve-year-old boy who looked like he'd just escaped from an orphanage. He was barefoot with pants that didn't look hemmed so much as chewed off at the bottom and a hole-infested tee shirt that read "Put a Tiger in Your Tank" in Spanish. I'd seen better ensembles in "Papillion."

Turned out he was quite a bit older and was the stevedore (short-hop LACSA planes didn't have flight attendants). His name, which took me forever to understand, was Constantinopolis. Conti could carry prodigious loads of cargo prodigious distances and never sweat, never get tired and never lose his smile. He talked all the time, and while I realized we both were speaking Spanish, it was clear we weren't speaking the same language. It was almost like a guy learning English in Bombay and talking to somebody from Alabama. Listening to Conti gave me my first clue that my struggles with Spanish would be taking on an added dimension.

We flew very low over the astonishingly verdant landscape, sailing just a few hundred feet above the jungle canopy. In the clearings I could plainly see cattle look up and those big white cowbirds rise and resettle as our plane droned overhead.

I was glad to see cattle. They were just about the only things that looked familiar. Even the trees looked different. From above they didn't look like trees; they looked like giant broccoli, so thick you couldn't see the trunks, just the tops. We followed the rivers a lot and I was amazed how tall the trees were, thirty to forty feet high, battling each other for supremacy in the sunlight, most of them dangling vines that would have warmed Tarzan's heart.

Just before we made our final turn for San Isidro, I got my first glimpse of Lake Nicaragua in the distance. I thought many times later how close the lake looked on my first day, and how incredibly, muddily, shark-and-crocodile-infested distant it seemed every day I spent on the ground.

We had to make two passes at the San Isidro airstrip. The airstrip doubled as a cattle grazing area and the lumbering Brahmas were reluctant, or too filled with ennui (19) to yield territory. The DC3 buzzed them, scattering the cowbirds in every direction, and then floated down to what I had to admit was a very soft and expert landing.

When Conti opened the plane's big side door, the moist jungle heat came rushing in and grabbed me by the throat. I was actually having a hard time breathing, made worse by the fact that I was wearing my tan Panama suit, white long-sleeved shirt and narrow black tie. I was determined to make a good impression on the townspeople.

Who were nowhere in sight.

I stood stupidly at the bottom of the little ramp when I saw a black man catching a mail pouch dropped by the pilot out of the plane's side window. He saw me and gave me a curious smile.

He walked up to me and held out his hand. In a California-tinged accent he said, "If your name is Jack Harjo (he pronounced it "Are-show," as would everybody else in Costa Rica), you're not supposed to be here till Friday. The school kids were planning a big parade and everything. Well, hell."

I gave him a sweaty palm that was the result of humidity and apprehension. "In that case, do you think it would be okay to loosen my tie?"

He laughed. "And take off that coat. Well, hell, where are my manners? I'm Mickey Munoz, the LACSA agent and telegraph operator. Seriously, we had a big shindig planned for you. Come on into the radio shack. It's a little cooler in there; at least it's out of the sun. I better radio don Victor. You want a Fanta? I got my own icebox."

Actually the radio shack felt hotter than outside. It reminded me of that corrugated tin coop where they put Alec Guinness in "Bridge on the River Kwai." I took my bottle of orange soda to a large shade tree and sat numbly on one of the sacks of beans Conti was unloading, looking and not looking at the Brahmas and their cowbird sidekicks who had reclaimed the pasture.

I could hear Mickey working the radio. "Calling don Victor, calling don Victor. Your man is here. Repeat, your man is in San Isidro. *Que sorpresa, verdad?*"

"*Your man?*" What the hell did that mean? It was too hot to think, so I just stared at the coat in my lap that had soaked completely through.

I really don't know how many minutes passed; shock can do that to you. But eventually I saw a man on a horse galloping across the pasture and up the gravelly runway directly toward me. He was wearing one of those funny canvas hats with the big floppy brims that Costa Rican farmers wear, so I couldn't make out his face until he was right on me. Then I thought perhaps I was hallucinating.

He leaped nimbly from his horse before it had completed its skidding stop. "Jack Harjo, my friend. Welcome. Now we can play Ticos and Indians." He laughed and grabbed me by the shoulders.

"Victor Victorin?" I was so stunned I could actually hear my own voice echoing in my ear as if part of me was outside listening in. "I can't say you are the last person on earth I expected to see, but you sure make the top one hundred. What in the hell are you doing here?"

He put his arm around me and guided me back to the shade tree. "Have a seat. Actually I live here, Jack. Well, sort of, near here and San Jose. My family owns two big *fincas* around here—one of cacao only a couple of miles away and our coffee plantation in the highlands where I spend most of my time. I'm glad you have come, Jack my friend. I know you are going to like it. At least I hope so, because I'm the reason you're here. I always liked you, Jack. When I got back to San Jose, I asked Mr. Le Pommes if you could run our baseball league, and he jumped at the chance. Come on, let's go to town. We've got you set up at a pension right by the river. You can rest up today. Tomorrow you will meet the mayor and the head of the civil guard and we'll give the children a chance to have their parade." He patted me on the back. "By the way, the mayor's a woman and very pretty. You can thank me later."

CHAPTER 17

San Isidro was (is?) a riparian (83) village that meandered for about a mile along the Zappo River. Zappo is the Spanish word for frog, which you might think is an ugly name for a river until you saw some of the frogs over here: brilliant crimson and lemon beauties only as big as your thumb that sounded as big as cocker spaniels when they started croaking at night. Come to think of it, everything—frogs, parrots, monkeys—were smaller and made more noise than the regular animals I had seen in zoos. Even the people were kind of short, wiry and tough as a boot.

The entire village was really two long streets that came out of the cacao trees and coffee plantations upstream and ended with a little Catholic church that somebody had painted silver. Once you paint something silver, by the way, you have to keep right on painting it silver, because no other paint will mask the original. I'm just telling you this in case you're thinking of painting your house silver. Not a bad color, I guess, but you damn well better like it. Just trying to be helpful.

My "office," the headquarters of the Northern Costa Rican Baseball League and the Ticolandia Farmers' Co-op, was a little two-room wooden building with a corrugated tin roof not far from the church. It had been built as a medical clinic, but the long-promised government doctor never showed up, so it just sat there waiting for the jungle to claim it. When Frank Le Pommes made his one visit to San Isidro before I got there, he said the Peace Corps wanted to rent space for the volunteer. "We have just the thing for you," Melba the Mayor said, "A former doctor's office."

"They seem perfect," Frank said in Spanish that would have made John McNaughton proud. "We have a doctor who can fly. How many moneys?"

"Well, it is a medical building with electricity," Melba the Mayor said, thinking on her feet. She thought of a ridiculous sum. "Including the electricity and furniture (which turned out to be a desk and wooden filing cabinet), 500 *colones* a month." That was about 75 American dollars.

Unaware that he could have had any building in town, including the church, for that price, Frank quickly agreed. I therefore became not only San Isidro's first Peace Corps volunteer; I became its cash cow, at least during the rainy season when they couldn't get the cacao to market.

Actually San Isidro didn't have a rainy season. It had a dry season, which they called *La Temporada*, which lasted from March to May. Otherwise it rained pretty much every single day. But it wasn't a gloomy rain. It was prompt and dependable, a rain you could live with and around. It never rained in the mornings, which was when most of the work got done. Then around two every afternoon, with no fanfare, no thunder, no lightning, no wind, no warning, the skies would open and drop buckets of rain, giant drops that stung your face if you were unlucky or dumb enough to stand out in it. *This time it isn't going to stop*, you'd think, *this time babies will drown; this time we will be swept into the Zappo.*

Then as quickly as it came, the rain would disappear, leaving a residue of heat, humidity and mud puddles that everybody in town could dance around except me. I was always ankle-deep in mud.

I paid Mickey, who had tons of free time, to go with me as I interviewed people in and around the village to see how I could be helpful. I carried a large notebook with me and took copious notes, which not only helped me remember, it protected my cover.

Mickey told me I needed to create a cover story, because people were already starting to make up stories that I was a spy, or a priest (Peace Corps translates into Body of Peace in Spanish, no help at all), or a tax collector from some vague government or a crazy rich American. Mickey said that in every single case, the people would lie, and who could blame them? Ask a poor person how you can help, and he'll say give me money. That doesn't take a rocket scientist to figure.

So I became what I actually sort of was—a journalist who had been sent to write about life in the jungle for an American magazine. Mickey in his wisdom told the *campesinos* not to spend too much time talking about the bad things, that would scare the Americans away, but talk about the good things, the real things, our children, our dreams, why we live here, why we wouldn't live anywhere else, the best way to cook *gallo pinto.*

With Mickey as my interpreter and guide, both my Spanish and my understanding of the people increased remarkably. And what I learned just staggered me, and made me very angry.

This was the first time in my life I had encountered real poverty. There were poor people in Oklahoma, of course, especially some of the poor black people I saw with Clara Luper. But the poor country folks around Ardmore didn't sleep on the ground, didn't share one bowl and one spoon because that's all they had, didn't get dengue fever and elephantiasis, and where only two out of every three babies born would live to see their fifth birthday.

The people were incredibly poor, but wore their poverty with dignity. Most of the men were cacao cutters, working every day in the muddy cacao orchards wielding scimitar-like knives on long poles that cut the ten-inch-long pods off the trees and into the sacks the men slung over their shoulders. No one could avoid the mud in the orchards, and it was killer mud that ate away the bottoms of the men's pants and removed skin and toenails. So the men, every single one of them, wore cheap rubber goulashes to protect their feet. The goulashes seemed to come only in one size—too large. You could hear the men squish-squishing their way home from work almost as soon as you saw them.

Out on the little farms where most people lived nobody wore, or maybe owned, shoes. The women were always barefoot around the house, sweeping the dirt floors and chasing chickens from the kitchen (I started raising chickens right away as a way to connect with the people, and it worked; I know my chickens). Most of the women owned one pair of plastic Mary Janes for church (leather shoes mildewed faster than the rats could eat them) for the one Sunday a month the traveling priest brought his little motor boat up the Zappo from the cathedral in Managua.

There wasn't a diaper within fifty miles of San Isidro. Infants and toddlers wore shirts (always clean, always clean—they loved their babies) but no pants, sort of like Disney characters and just as cute.

The *campesinos* were very gracious to Mickey and me, often offering us coffee or, if they had it, a roll or a cookie along with a string of apologies that there wasn't more to offer. On Mickey's instructions, I always accepted what was offered, regardless of how simple the home or how poor the family, and ate or drank it on the spot, in absolute violation of Peace Corps best practices. I began to adore these toothless men and old-before-their-time women and their chubby babies, who the mothers often would hold up to me as if for benediction.

I think the villagers were just a little flattered that a journalist was interested in their opinions and would go to the trouble of writing them down. Word got around that I wasn't a spy or a priest, and they opened up.

They really did like where they lived, and they made up all sorts of fairy tales to convince me and themselves that they had chosen wisely. Yes, the mosquitoes here can be very bad, but all they do is bite. They don't have diseases like the ones in Canas or Liberia. Be careful over there. The water here is pure and sweet, but don't drink the water in Belen or Bijagua; their water will give you worms. But don't worry, if you get worms you can kill them with shots of *guaro* (the local white lightning) and *cibichi*. It was all nonsense, but it gave the people comfort, and they told me these things not to brag, but to protect me, sometimes confiding in me in whispers.

I decided to home in on the children. Had they ever seen a doctor? Had they been given their small pox shot? No, sir, the doctor is in Canas, and besides he is very expensive and besides there is no road until the dry season. And we are lucky, because there is no small pox here, only in Nicaragua.

Which was true about Nicaragua. There had been an outbreak in Granada, which greatly concerned the Peace Corps. So those of us on or near the Nicaraguan border got a visit from Dr. Ernest Spiegel, the "doctor who flies."

Dr. Ernie was a nice enough guy, a former Army doctor who galvanized his heart by cracking corny jokes nonstop. He flew into San Isidro with hundreds of doses of small pox vaccine and over two grueling non-stop days we used every one of them.

Mickey had promised the families that if they brought their children to the clinic (that's what we called it in Spanish) the children would get a lollypop. But these loving, caring parents needed no incentive; they loved their children and stood patiently in a line that snaked all the way behind the church, sometimes for hours.

Dr. Ernie and I were like machines. I'd usher the family in, swab the child's arm, Dr. Ernie would gently tap the arm with three or four passes of the needle while the children stoically averted their eyes, I'd hand them a lollypop and it was on to the next family.

When Dr. Ernie climbed on the old DC-3 the next afternoon, I was exhausted and just sat on the clinic's wooden floor, eating a candy bar and drinking a grape soda, staring out the back door into the post-rain dampness.

Then I recognized one of the young couples I had interviewed approaching the back door. The man and woman were both dressed as if they were going to church. In the woman's arms, wrapped in a light blanket, was a baby.

I stood at the door. "I'm sorry, but the doctor has gone," I said. "Perhaps he will return next month."

The woman, who looked no more than fifteen, handed the swaddled baby up to me. "My little son is sick, mister doctor. He has diarrhea (which she called the curse) and even though we have given him nothing for two days as the old grandmother told us, still he goes and goes. We cannot pay, but please give him medicine."

If only Dr. Ernie was still around, if only they'd come the day before.

I put the little boy gently on the desk. He was gray, the same color as the blanket. I was on dangerous ground, but as I looked down on the dehydrated child, I couldn't help it. "The grandmother was wrong. Your boy needs something in his stomach right now."

I mixed a chunk of the candy bar and grape soda into a paste and spooned it into his mouth. He sucked at it weakly, then he coughed twice, blew out a little puff of chocolaty breath and died.

I vainly tried to give the child artificial respiration by lifting and lowering his arms, but after a few minutes it was clear it was too late. I didn't know what to do. I dumbly handed the baby back to the mother, who with dry eyes covered his face with the blanket, turned and walked into the jungle. The husband shook my hand and bowed slightly. "Thank you, mister doctor. You are very kind." Then he, too, was gone.

I turned back to the desk and both hands began to shake violently. I wanted to get rid of the spoon, but I couldn't hold on and it rattled across the floor. I stared at it and made a silent pledge to do whatever it took to lift this crazy-ass yoke of poverty.

CHAPTER 18

A few nights later, Victor, Mickey and I got together in the corrugated tin LACSA office across the river from town. We sat on boxes drinking cold Imperial beers from Mickey's refrigerator and taking the occasional tug on a bottle of *Flor de Caña* rum. Mickey and Victor were smoking cigars, which put a poker-party haze over the light cast by the single 40-watt bulb. We weren't trying to get drunk, but we didn't give a shit either.

I inscribed a mark on the dirt floor with my boot. "I don't get it," I said. "Costa Rica is supposed to be a wealthy nation, all things considered. And I see the people here working like motherfuckers every single day—hard, dangerous work and still they don't have enough money to buy shoes, or see a doctor, or buy medicine for their children and the children fucking die, they just fucking die."

Mickey considered the large square brown bottle of Nicaraguan rum, and then took a swig. "The crazy and sad thing is that at least once a year, they do have money. They get fistfuls of it when the trucks finally arrive in the dry season and take the cacao to market. But it's hard to value something you've done without for nine months. How well I know that game. I was in the merchant marines for five years. Ever hear of "sailor rich?"

"You were in the merchant marines? No wonder your English is so darn good."

"Yeah, I was a radio man, based out of San Diego. Anyway, we'd go weeks, sometimes months at sea where the only time you even saw money was in a poker game. Food, laundry, your bunk—absolutely free. Then we'd get into port and they paid us on the spot, in cash. We were young and dumb and money had no meaning to us, really. I'd always send some home to San Isidro, but mostly I drank and whored it away. One time when we got back from a trip to Okinawa, I bought a motorcycle and wrecked it three days later. Just walked away and left it. People around here are kind of the same—young and dumb, at least uneducated and with no experience whatsoever with money. What food they don't grow they get from the grocer on credit, same thing goes for cloth for shirts and stuff. Then in April the man gets, I don't know, a thousand *colones,* he buys his wife a new dress for Easter, some toys for the kids, then he'll slip off to Los Chiles or Canas, buy a bottle of scotch that costs twice as much here as it does in the states, get falling-down drunk, maybe get laid, maybe get rolled, and then come back to cut cacao for another year. He looks around and everybody else is doing the same thing, so he figures okay that's what you do."

"That's why we need that *puta* co-op," Victor said. "The co-op could buy and store the cacao right here, pay the cutters a little something every month, loan them money for new teeth or maybe to plant some more trees or buy another cow, and teach them about budgets—make them smart about money."

"You are the damndest communist I've ever met," I said, relieving Mickey of the bottle. "I've heard that one of the biggest buyers of cacao is your family's company. Wouldn't a co-op be in direct competition with your family's business?"

"Social democrat, remember?" Victor answered. "And it's not really my family's business. Not anymore. The only thing family about it now is the name. When my father died, his brother—I refuse to respect him enough to call him my uncle—bought, stole and cheated my sisters and me out of our birthright. I was in the university in Buenos Aires when my father died. My poor mother, who still lives in San Jose, didn't know any more about money than Mickey's sailors. So that bastard bought her out for pennies, set her up in a nice house, and promised her there would always be a place for us, his family, in the family business. When I got back to Costa Rica, I found there was a place for me in the business, all right—directly under his shoe. But the man is evil, not stupid. He made me many promises at first, promises of money, promises about positions in the company, but also promises about a career in politics. Costa Rica is a small country, Jack. A smart man with money and a recognized name can go far here, maybe to the president's office. I saw the dream for social democracy for my little country becoming a reality, so I took a bite of Eden's apple. I ate from the money tree.

"Now I have nice clothes, an apartment in San Jose, a Toyota Land Cruiser, and, I discovered, a poisoned career in politics. My father's brother whispered to many of the right people in government and the press that, as much as it pains him to say so, I cannot be trusted. He used my well-known friendship with Che to suggest that I am a pawn of Castro, and would hand him our country on a platter if I got the chance. But do not worry, he says, he will watch over me. What is family for, after all? So I can't get a job in government, I can't get a job anywhere else, and I get sick to my heart when I see Victorin Limited taking bread out of the mouths of these poor people.

"Do I think the co-op will be in competition with the Victorin company? Yes, dear God, I hope so. The co-op is social democracy in action. And if it will also deliver a blow to my father's brother, so much the better." He put his cigar in his mouth in a jaunty angle I had seen Guevara do in a newsreel a few years back.

"Speaking of this mysterious and wondrous co-op, where is it?" I asked. "Canas, Liberia? I sure as hell can't find any traces of it."

Victor laughed and tapped his cigar against his temple. "Right up here. I made it up so we could convince the Peace Corp that we had plenty of work to keep a volunteer busy. The baseball league is pretty much a fiction, too, although we do play baseball, especially the Nicaraguans. I filed all the proper papers with Mayor Melba, who agreed they were both good ideas, and together we sent a proposal to your new boss, what's his name, La Palma. He's a very trusting man, your boss. When he arrived here, we even had a baseball game going on the soccer field. We told him it was a league game. He actually clapped his hands. So here you are, Jack."

Mickey stared thoughtfully into the rum bottle and sprinkled the last few drops onto his tongue. Then he smiled at the ceiling in a way that made his gold-encrusted teeth sparkle against his mahogany skin. "Think of it this way—no bad habits to break."

CHAPTER 19

The co-op may have been a fantasy, but the young men of the region had a love of baseball that was very real. This was especially true of the Nicaraguans who had come down to work the cacao and rice plantations. Nicaraguans were nuts about baseball.

Nicaragua actually had its own class double-A baseball league. The men knew their baseball and baseball players. A lot of major leaguers on their way up or down passed through Nicaragua. For some reason, it was a former New York Met named Marvin Throneberry who captured the Nicaraguan fancy, perhaps because he was the whitest white man any of them had ever seen. Everywhere I went the men would ask me if I knew Marvin Throneberry. "Marvelous Marv" Throneberry, also known as the Mets' Dr. Strangeglove, spent his final, alcohol-laced two years in baseball as the first baseman for the Managua Tigers. Yes, I said to their open-mouthed joy, I know him, and Sandy Koufax and Al Kaline and Roger Maris and Mickey Mantle, who came from Oklahoma just like me. He was older than I was or we might have played together, I added, fibbing without really fibbing.

But I damn well did know my baseball, better even than my chickens, and a hell of a lot better than anybody else in northern Costa Rica. So with Mickey Munoz's help I formed a league (my Spanish was improving by leaps and bounds, but some of the baseball lingo stumped me. Outfielders in Spanish are called gardeners, for example. One look at our shabby baseball field told me ours should have been called harvesters).

With the exception of a few wet baseballs that dried rock-hard and some bats, some with chips out of them, we had no equipment. So I wrote a letter to Mr. James at OTABCO asking if they could send some old American Legion gloves and balls and caps. He wrote back and said he wouldn't send them, but he would bring them. He and his wife had always wanted to visit Costa Rica, he said, and see the quaint painted carts and coffee trees and volcanoes and stuff. I didn't have the heart to tell him that we were way short on carts and volcanoes, but we did have Victor's coffee plantation and jungles and monkeys and parrots, so I thought I could keep him busy.

Two weeks later Mickey handed me a telegram double-folded and sealed with an official-looking stamp. I took it apprehensively.

"What does it say?" I asked. "Did something bad happen?"

"You pain me," Mickey said in mock solemnity. "You know I just transcribe and paste. It's just words to me. But if I had read it, it probably would say that your baseball teams just won the Irish Sweepstakes. Your fat cat from Oklahoma and his wife are arriving in San Isidro on next Thursday's LACSA flight loaded with baseball equipment. That's just a guess, you understand."

After the ceremonial buzzing of the cattle to clear the field, the LACSA DC-3 landed right on schedule. The first thing I noticed when the door swung open was little Constantinopolis sporting an Ardmore Pirates baseball cap and an Oklahoma City Indians tee shirt. He hopped out of the plane, grabbed a twine-trussed cardboard box the size of a refrigerator and crab-walked it to Mickey's office, where I was waiting. I walked out with Mickey as he pushed the stairs into place.

Mr. James appeared at the top step sweating bullets. He spotted me and waved. "Good God Almighty, Jack. Nobody told us you worked in a steam bath. San Jose was so pleasant. Get us to someplace air conditioned, okay? The missus isn't looking all that good for wear."

I kind of figured this might happen, so I hustled them across the river as quickly as I could to the cavernous pension *Buena Vista*, whose open-air bar/restaurant was built right over a bend in the river and picked up what breezes there were.

Mr. and Mrs. James were the first real grown-up Americans the villagers had ever seen and they treated them like royalty, or aliens from outer space. The children, whose jungle telegraph was extraordinary, showed up out of nowhere and hid in every corner, peeking over windowsills and railings, dozens of giggling eyes (well, I know eyes don't giggle, but if they did, those would have) hoping to see something awesome or better yet, monstrous.

Doña Margarita, who owned the pension, and her three daughters brought plate after plate of things to nibble on, what the locals called *bocas*—hearts of palm with a dollop of mayonnaise on top, Vienna sausages speared by toothpicks, bits of crumbly goat cheese on a Costa Rican version of Ritz crackers, and my favorite, fried plantains.

Mrs. James sat dumbly at the oilcloth-covered table overlooking the river, staring into her grape Fanta, eating nothing and wishing herself onto an ice floe in the Antarctic. Mr. James, on the other hand, though still sweating, had a robust appetite and seemed to be regaining his footing. He had a beer in one hand and whatever food was being offered in the other, which he used for a pointer as he paced back and forth like a hippo on Dexedrine.

"You know, Jack, this isn't so bad once you get used to it, huh? Kind of Tarzan-y. Look over there, Doris, there's a monkey in the kitchen. I think that's the kitchen. There's nothing out here that can eat us, is there?" This monologue was accompanied by guffaws, snorts and extravagant gestures that made me cringe, but delighted the children.

Shortly Constantinopolis, whose tee shirt was perspiration-free as usual, showed up with the enormous box, accompanied by Mayor Melba. Mayor Melba was neither as young nor as pretty as Victor had advertised, but she was attractive in a school-marmy kind of way, and like Constantinopolis never seemed to break a sweat. I used to look at her with her hair neatly piled up, her crisp cotton blouses and her single strand of pearls around her neck and think she must have stumbled onto the wrong movie set—Jungle Jim instead of Marjorie Morningstar.

Mayor Melba approached Mr. James as if she were approaching a visiting foreign head of state. Mr. James was busily popping some of the twine with a buck knife that had drawn gasps of admiration from the children when he opened it.

Mayor Melba handed Mr. James something that might have been a scroll tied in a red ribbon. "Welcome to San Isidro," she said in flawless unaccented English. Then she turned to me and shrugged sheepishly. "I am afraid that is about all my English, Jack. You need to help me."

Mr. James got wrapped up in the pomp of the moment. "On behalf of the people of Ardmore, Oklahoma and the Oklahoma Tire, Auto . . . what?"

Mayor Melba's eyes grew large as she gazed over Mr. James' shoulder. Then breaking all protocol, she pushed her way past him. "Jack, tell him that his wife has fainted," she shouted.

I ran into the kitchen for a wet cloth, while Mr. James spun and with surprising grace for a man his size, dropped to his knees, grabbed his wife's hand and started patting it. "Oh, hell and damn, Dori, wake up. Don't die on me, girl. Not here, not now."

Mrs. James slowly sat upright with Mayor Melba's help, placing the wet dish cloth I handed her to her forehead. She let out an exasperated breath. "Let me know where and when, okay, Dwight?" she said in a voice usually reserved for pets. "I wasn't dying. I was just resting my face on the oil cloth. First cool thing I've felt since we got here." She turned to me. "And young man, with all due respect, I don't want to be here anymore. I don't understand this machine-gun language, I don't like monkeys, I'm miserable and I'm getting back on that airplane, with or without you, Mr. Big Shot."

"Yes, dear," Mr. James said. He turned to me. "Run tell them to hold the plane, Jack. We'll be along in a minute." I knew there was no real hurry, because Mickey was standing next to Constantinopolis, and the plane wasn't going anywhere without them. But I told Conti to run to the plane anyway. I didn't want Mr. James to have a heart attack on top of everything else.

The big sweet-hearted fat man looked sadly down at the partially-opened cardboard box. "There's a bunch of good stuff in there," he said. "I'd hoped to open it with you. I even had a speech and everything. But I'm with Mrs. James on this one. I don't know how in the hell you can play baseball in this shit, no disrespect, ma'am." He nodded to Mayor Melba, who had no idea what he was saying.

When Mickey and I returned from the air strip fifteen minutes later, Mayor Melba and what seemed like half the women and children in town were pulling things out of the box and laying them respectfully in piles on the floor. There were four catcher's mitts and masks, at least a dozen gloves, including, I noted, a left-handed first baseman's mitt for me. There were boxes of balls, including the rubber-covered practice balls that would be great for rainy days, a dozen bats, a pile of Ardmore Pirates caps, and Oklahoma City Indians tee shirts. Mayor Melba held up a gray cotton short-sleeved shirt that I recognized instantly. It was one of the OTABCO Treaders uniforms. Sure enough, when she turned it around, it had OTABCO stitched in blue across the back.

She looked at me curiously. "What does this word mean?"

"It's my old baseball team. It's not really a word, just letters that in English represent the name of a tire and auto supply company in Oklahoma."

Mayor Melba laughed heartily. "Well, I was thinking in Spanish. And I was thinking you ordered these shirts for your new league. I couldn't understand at first, then I thought 'Aha—*Organizacion Tico de Beisbol Co-Operativa*'. OTABCO." She waved the shirt like a matador's cape.

I actually clapped my hands like Frank Le Pommes. "That's it," I shouted.

And thus was born the company that would put me on the cover of *Newsweek* magazine, then dash the cup of fame from my lips and send me packing to Bluefields with a price on my head. Still a good idea, all and all.

CHAPTER 20

The Tico Baseball Co-Op was only days out of Mayor Melba's mouth when I was called to Peace Corps headquarters to describe it.

Once a quarter we'd get together in San Jose for Frank's sunny attaboys and Dr. Ernie's gamma globulin shots that felt like little dollops of fire in your back side. Then we'd try to impress each other with our works in progress.

Our first meeting was dominated by the city volunteers whose jobs had been spelled out from the start. Walt Connelly was teaching science and math at a suburban high school, exactly what he'd been doing in Grand Rapids the year before; Jeannie Carter and Katy Babcock, both who had teetered dangerously on the edge of becoming nuns themselves, were working at the Catholic orphanage in Cartago, supervising the lunches while the nuns taught school and prepared dinner. Jeannie said they made so many cheese sandwiches that she was convinced Cartago was where surplus American cheese went to die. Bilingual Tom Bach taught English at the University of Costa Rica and had already been featured in *La Prensa* as an example of Peace Corps competency.

Then there were guys like John McNaughton, Collette Johnson and me. We were what the ever-euphemistic Peace Corps called "community development specialists," meaning that neither our villages nor PC headquarters knew what to do with us, but were hoping we'd think of something.

So Frank really surprised me when in October he asked me how things were going in San Isidro. "What a lovely jungle setting," Frank effused. "I bet someone could open one of those safari hotels like Helen and I visited in Tanganyika. All very Stanley and Livingston, with those dugout canoes down the river and everything. Charming, just charming."

Yeah, right. Maybe we could call it the Doris James Last Resort, you dumb fuck. All right, you asked for it. Stanley and Livingston, my ass. I stood so I could literally think on my feet. I was going to make it up as I went along.

"Well, our goals aren't quite that lofty, but we do have a fledgling co-op and savings organization that just might take some of the sting out of the grinding poverty in the area. Because there are no roads in or out of San Isidro nine months of the year, the cacao workers can't get their product to market, and when the road finally does open up, the unscrupulous buyers swoop in, hand the workers a wad of money that looks good if you've been without it for half a year, and ride off with the cacao, laughing all the way. We think the co-op could help break that cycle of poverty."

There was a low murmur of approval from the volunteers, some of whom had last seen me standing alone with my foot locker of books and a mosquito net.

Frank's eyes, which were already too close together for my taste, squinted in concentration. "But I thought you were going to start a baseball league," he said in a semi-question, leaving the sentence dangling in the air like a teen-ager.

"We're using the league as the base," I said. "That will give us local co-ops in each of the six towns in the league. In fact, we're combining the two. We're calling it OTABCO, the *Organizacion Tico de Beisbol Co-Operativa.*" Tom Bach clapped his hands at this, making me wonder if it was catching.

"Now Jack, old man, you know we're just here to help." Frank was starting to sound like Robert Donat in "Goodbye Mr. Chips," and it was a little annoying. "Sounds like you have taken the lead on this project and that won't do, as interesting as it might be."

"Absolutely not," I lied. "The enterprise is headed up by San Isidro's mayor, Melba Marenco. You met her on your visit, remember?"

"A fine woman—very level-headed; but you mentioned five other towns. Will the mayor of one town be welcomed as a leader in the others? Do you have any evidence that it can even get off the ground?"

Frank was truly beginning to piss me off. I knew it was hard for him to trot out his Harvard business degree when you're talking about cheese sandwiches at orphanages, but he was putting me through the wringer just to show everybody how smart he was. I almost laughed as I paid silent homage to my late mother.

"Absence of evidence is not evidence of absence, boss," I answered as politely as I could. "That's where the baseball teams come in. Each town team manager has agreed to serve as co-op coordinator. It's a perfect fit." I made a mental note to visit the team managers the minute I got back to San Isidro and clue them in. I figured they'd say yes, if for no other reason than they got to wear those neat OTABCO jerseys.

"Sounds like you've thought of just about everything," Frank said and gave me a steely glare that suggested he knew I was lying.

John McNaughton saved my bacon by chiming in. "I think that's just the ticket, Jack, old man. We need one of those down in bananaville where I'm working. The American Fruit Company is just stepping on the throats of the growers down there. If we had a co-op we could do the same thing you're doing with cacao. Will you help me get started? And one more question—where are you getting the money? Co-ops are all about money and I understand raising initial capital can be a bitch."

"Who you calling a bitch?" Collette laughed as she rose to her feet. I knew the idea must have moved her; she always stood when she really wanted you to listen. "It wouldn't take a lot of money, I bet. A co-op is a fantastic idea for the women's clubs I am starting in Limon. Even very little loans could make a big difference to my women. Ten dollars for a bolt of cloth, twenty-five dollars for a sewing machine, a dollar for buttons and zippers—those gals could pay back the money in no time, and there's no way on earth they could get a loan any other way. Jack, my friend, you've just come up with what we used to call in Chicago an RBFI—really big fucking idea. We need a co-op in the worst way. Maybe we can join yours?"

I had been thinking about this non-stop since Victor and Mickey and I had hashed the co-op out over sips of rum. Now that I had John and Collette watching my back, I thought there was no time like the present to get the dough we needed.

"Well, there's no reason why we couldn't work together, now that you mention it. We could share accounting, filing and back room expenses at least," I said.

"Not to mention loan fulfillment and re-insurance," John said. John's comments added weight to the conversation; being a business school grad from Brown, he was the only one of us who actually knew what the hell he was talking about. "But again the question: it may not take a lot of money, but it is going to take some money. I'd ball-park that less than $10,000 could get us kicked off. So where do we get it?"

I'm afraid the idea of actually helping those poor, dear people and their dying babies got me carried away. I had forgotten that John wasn't the only one in the room with a business school background.

I turned to Frank. "What do you say, boss? You'd have three volunteers working together, it seems like a pretty low risk-to-reward project, it's clearly community development through and through, and it wouldn't cost a lot. Can we get a loan from the Peace Corps to get it started?"

It was clear that Frank had been stung by my "absence of evidence" remark and he was ready to pounce. "Low risk, huh? If you knew anything about credit unions, granges and co-ops, which you obviously don't, you would know that in the United States, for every one that succeeds, another fails. And Costa Rica, I'm sure you've noticed, isn't the United States.

"But even if I had ten thousand dollars in my pocket, which I don't, the Peace Corps wouldn't let me give it to you. Gang, the only capital Peace Corps volunteers have access to is human capital, and our only equity is sweat equity. If there is even a hint villagers can get money from you guys, your lives will be miserable and your mission compromised. You are volunteer co-workers, not Daddy Warbucks. Stick with your baseball, Jack." He brightened up. "And don't forget the jungle safari deal Helen and I thought about. You don't need any money for that, just a dugout canoe."

* * *

I had been standing through this entire diatribe, and that "dugout canoe" comment just fried me. I spun on my heels and walked out of the conference room straight to Oldimar's Bar Soda Palace. I had barely gotten seated when John and Collette came running up to my table.

"That was the most bullshit disrespectful fucking display of Big Boss Man ass-holedness I've ever witnessed," John semi-shouted as he threw himself into a chair. His always ruddy complexion had turned vermillion.

"Do you know that he simply left me standing there?" Collette was fuming, too. "Then he turned to Jerry and asked him if there was anything going on in Limon that didn't require a loan. I couldn't believe it. The only thing Jerry has made since we got there is that whore at the Blue Parrot. So I plucked John's sleeve and we followed you out. The co-op is such a good idea, Jack. Well, at least you got yours up and running. I'm just sorry that we can't join you."

Oldimar came over with three banana splits and slid them in front of us. "Wow, the new Peace Corps—mad and loud. No new dirty words in here, okay, John? What's the matter, boy from Oklahoma? Your dog die?"

I just stared at the three sagging swirls of almost-ice cream. I talked to my banana split. "It is a good idea. And it could work." I lifted my eyes to look at Collette. "But to be honest, it's still in idea phase in San Isidro, too. I'm working on it, but Frank surprised me and pissed me off as usual, so I, um, embellished things a little."

"How little?" John asked.

"Every bit of it except the name. That we got from a tire supply company in Oklahoma that sent me some baseball uniforms."

We sat there glumly eating our banana splits as other volunteers came pouring into the restaurant, the meeting clearly broken up. They approached our table in clusters of three and four, quietly expressing platitudinous condolences. We felt like the surviving family members at a funeral. For some reason this reminded me of my mother's memorial, and my hair-trigger Creek temper got the best of me.

"Well, fuck Frank Le Pommes," I said finally. "And fuck the Peace Corps, if it comes to that. Frank has never held a dying baby in his arms. This co-op idea can work and will work. If we can scrape the money together, are you guys still willing to work with me on it?"

"God, yes," John said. "Count me in. I'd like to leave a legacy a little more indelible that teaching Dick and Jane and Spot and Fluffy to kids who couldn't give a shit. What about it Collette?"

She hesitated just a beat. "I think so, but I need to check with my women. I also need to bring Jerry in; he can't help, but he could hurt. I'll let you know. But we get back to John's original question: where are we going to get the money? If we go to USAID, Frank will scuttle us for sure."

I smiled. "We don't need USAID and we don't need Frank Le Fucking Pommes. In some ways I may represent Frank's worst nightmare."

John leaned forward. "What's that? An intelligent man?"

"Nope—an Indian with a trust fund. I'm going to find the money. Let's get together tomorrow morning and map out next steps. I'm going back to the hotel, send a few telegrams, then go to bed. I'm bushed." I turned to Collette. "Let me know as soon as you can if you can be a part of this. I'd like that."

A few hours later I heard a faint knocking on my hotel room door. I opened it to find a smiling and slightly out-of-breath Collette Johnson.

"Well, that was fast," I said. "Is it good news?"

Her smile broadened into a sunlit grin. Maybe I hadn't really noticed how pretty she was under that street-wise façade. "I hope you think so. Actually I haven't talked with Jerry yet. But I'm proud of you, Jack. For the second time in a year, I'm really proud of you, and I didn't even know who you were when I carried that 'Waiting for a Hamburger' editorial around in my bill-fold. So I was thinking: an RBFI deserves an RBF. What do you say? You're not too tired are you?"

My voice involuntarily dropped half an octave and got scratchy. "No, absolutely not," I said. "Please come in and close the door behind you."

CHAPTER 21

If you are like me and tend to skip over the mushy parts in books, then this is the part you might want to skip over.

I want to talk about Collette, because I flat fell in love with that girl.

My experience in love is obviously limited. Glinda was just a place-holder for me, as I guess I was for her, crawling over each other's teen-age bodies like Margaret Mead in New Guinea, full of wonder and discovery.

Judy was a different matter entirely. Judy was so much smarter and more sophisticated than I was that I was filled with awe, an awe I equated with love, the way a nine-year-old falls in love with his third-grade teacher. And Judy was pretty, in that Katharine Hepburn touch-but-not-too-much sort of way.

Then here came Collette, who was Judy turned inside-out in almost every conceivable way. Judy wore her righteous indignation against the treatment of blacks, women, the poor and whatever group was next in line as a thin candy shell around her heart, like an M & M. And that was sure one M & M that wasn't going to melt in your hands.

Collette, on the other hand, wore every emotion on her sleeve. She invited you in to her heart and her head, and wrapped you in her embrace when you accepted. She was a hugger, and I guess when she was little, that was about all she had to give.

Collette was very pretty, but she had a beauty that crept up on you. She had a sunny, picnic face that you thought about later and liked even better. She had green, curious eyes and a slight gap between her front teeth that added to her playfulness. She had a country smile and a sassy city street-wise mouth, irresistible to my way of thinking.

As she discussed openly in the articles she wrote for *Ladies Home Journal,* Collette was born church mouse-poor on the south side of Chicago. Poverty swirled around her ankles as a child the way jimson weed did mine. Poverty was a concept to Judy, and she despised it. When Collette looked into poverty's mirror, she saw her own reflection and she stuck out her tongue and laughed.

Collette laughed at everything—a lean back your head and let her rip laugh that was so honest and infectious I've actually seen people half-way across a restaurant laugh with her simply because her laughter gave them pleasure.

She even laughed when we made love, and giggled, and sang, and talked, and whispered, and wept. And when she had an orgasm, people halfway across a restaurant . . . just joking, but you get the idea. She was such a robust lover, so generous and caring, and finally she would have what she called the climax of the gods. Her climaxes would sometimes draw me into a climax of my own, out of the pure joy of being part of hers.

And by the way, Collette and I made love; Judy and I had sex. Comparisons really aren't fair, of course, and old love affairs look smaller in the rear view mirror, but the barb of rejection had gone deeper than I thought, and Collette was balm.

Being in love with Collette wasn't easy on several levels. The Peace Corps from Sargent Shriver right on down was very Catholic, very cautious and bordered on the prudish. Volunteers assigned to the same village who seemed too chummy quickly found themselves in new assignments hundreds of miles apart. A volunteer named Vickie Reyes fell in love with a local school teacher and was sent home so fast and so quietly most of us didn't know she was gone for weeks.

So Collette and I were careful.

We'd find ways to be in San Jose at the same time, sometimes officially, sometimes just a sneak. We'd stay in the hotel the Peace Corps had arranged for us and make love in another, if for no other reason than the fact that Collette's high-volume orgasms would have given us away. Later, Victor let us use his apartment near the airport that even had its own Toyota Land Cruiser, but there was something kind of backstreet delicious about the early rendezvous sites.

My favorite times were when we'd take the bus to the busy little Pacific port town of Puntarenas. Puntarenas had no Peace Corps volunteers, so it was safe. It was a town full of strangers, with tons of sports fishermen and the occasional cruise ship, so Collette and I blended in with the crowd. I'd wear a baseball cap and Collette found a wide-brimmed straw hat that just screamed tourist. We'd walk along the quay, looking at junk jewelry, tee shirts and sandals, eating ceviche and being in love.

Thanks to our co-conspirator Oldimar, we found a bungalow on the beach near a sports-fishing wharf south of town. The fishermen were all up at daybreak and out to sea, so we had the run of the beach for most of the day. We'd walk up and down the silvery-gray beach looking for sand dollars and listening to the jungle birds and monkeys only yards away. Sometimes as we sat reading or writing letters, boys from town would come by selling mangoes on sticks or papayas with juicy limes. Those were the best times I ever knew.

Our favorite restaurant was a palm-thatched open-air joint called Mariscos del Sol. The owner, whose name was Celso, knew Oldimar, of course, and took us under his wing. He told us to keep our eyes peeled because sometimes famous people would show up. Ernest Hemingway and his friends come, Celso said, and sometimes John Wayne. "But not side by side, no way, Jose. One time yes, but not now. Papa gets drunk one night and calls Mister Wayne 'Mount Baldy.' Mister Wayne gets mad and says 'How is your brother Fidel?' 'Still sleeping with your sister,' says Papa. Papa was lucky there was a man with a camera from the boat. Mr. Wayne's bodyguards pulls him away fast, or Papa goes to sleep, I think. Mr. Wayne sure is big." Celso laughed. "Bur Papa had reason: Mr. Wayne is bald as a football." I marveled that not only were Celso and Oldimar friends, they seemed to have attended the same foreign language school.

My favorite dish from Celso was a grilled sea bass served whole and sitting on its stomach and pelvic fins like it was ready to swim off the plate. I could never get Collette to join me. "I make it a rule not to eat things that look at me while I'm doing it," she said.

"We Indians think the eye is the window to the soul," I teased. "We eat the eye and head first, so we can understand and honor our kill."

She stared at me deadpan. "That is one of the most repulsive stories I've ever heard. Remind me never to have a steak with you. And mister, unless you can find some mouthwash in town, the kissing lamp is off until further notice."

The other reason we were circumspect was because Collette was black and I was, um, non-black, and our being together was just as unusual in certain parts of Costa Rica as it was back in the states. Ironically our skin was exactly the same color. Ironically, too, I remember being in New Orleans with Judy where I was afraid the police would mistake me for black. In Costa Rica I was kind of hoping people would do just that.

We talked about this a lot. It was often post-coital bedtime conversation that made the subject more dream-like and less threatening. "Do you think your father would approve of us being together?" She asked me on one of our first trips to Puntarenas.

"Well, I might have to do some back hoeing," I admitted. "I wrote Daddy that you went to SMU, so he thinks you're a rich Texan. I think he'll be so relieved to find you aren't from Texas, you'll be home free. Isn't it silly? I still call him Daddy. What do you call your father?"

"Long gone." There was no laughter at this obvious punch line and the delivery was too polished. There was pain there, so I just kept silent.

"I never met my father," she said with an enormous sigh. "To be brutally honest, I'm not sure my mother could pick him out of a line-up. My mother had a number of gentlemen callers, as Tennessee Williams called them, and they occasionally left a baby behind. I got two brothers, one older, one younger. My older brother's last name is Thomas, and I don't remember seeing Mr. Thomas around the house, either. It's a ghetto thing."

"It's a long way from the south side of Chicago to Southern Methodist, I imagine," I prompted in another nighttime conversation.

"I was part of an experiment, just like we are now," she said, lightly tapping my chest in time to a song only she could hear. "Mother has never run a very tight ship, bless her heart, so I sort of became my own mother. I worked after school, damn near lived in the public library, made good grades and plotted my escape. Then the McNamara Foundation offered me a full-boat scholarship as part of their plan to integrate southern colleges. I said hell yeah. Know why I picked SMU?" She gave that bubble-over laugh. "It wasn't the Deep South, and I figured Methodists wouldn't shoot you. But God takes care of fools and little children. SMU turned out to be good choice—a small college in a ritzy suburb of Dallas.

"Truth be told, I just sort of went through the paces in college. I was marking time, didn't even declare a major until my senior year. I hadn't really gone to SMU as much as I had escaped the South Side. Then comes my senior year, my scholarship is about to peter out, I know I can never go back to Chicago, *Ladies Home Journal* said thanks but no thanks when I asked about a job there, so I started hatching another escape plan. I applied to the Peace Corps. I figured it would at least give me a two-year breather. But I got more than I bargained for. I got you guys. You were all card-carrying optimists, full of life, as far removed from my childhood as was humanly possible. And I got you."

I asked her if working with poor women reminded her too much of the old days. "No, sweets, not at all," she answered. "In fact, I'm grateful to find out that poor comes in different shapes and sizes. I was used to that dull gray, hang around the liquor store, hopeless, grinding poverty of the inner city. Did you know that my older brother had already done six months in juvie for hot-wiring cars by the time he was fifteen? He'll never get out of the ghetto. But I'm going to make sure my little brother does, even if I have to carry him out of there on my back.

"When I got to Limon I found, yeah, that the women in my sewing circles didn't have any money. They had that kind of poverty going for them. But they didn't have the poverty of the spirit I saw back home. These women, their eyes were bright, they'd laugh and dance and cuddle their babies. They'd cook and sing and chirp like birds. And hard work? Holy shit. All they needed was a little help in getting their business off the ground, and I discovered I could give that to them. And they needed a little money.

"That's why I jumped out of my seat when I heard you talking about the co-op. I knew instantly that it was right for me and my ladies—maybe more right for us than for your farmers. We've just got to do this, Jack. I don't have two nickels to rub together, but I have a little something I can offer. For some reason Frank Le Pommes doesn't like you. But he's scared of me; I can smell it. If you can find some money, I can handle Frank. That's my ante."

"Then pot's right, my little longhorn. Let's go down to Golfito and bring John along."

CHAPTER 22

The first honest-to-god letter I ever got from my father was also one of the most important.

"I've talked your idea of a farmers' co-op over with the Ag agent here in Ardmore," his letter said in part, "As well as some fellows down at the grange hall, and they all think this is a very good idea. So we are going to invest in your venture, son. And when I say we, I mean me and Dwight James. He's done nothing but talk about you since he got back from your village. He said anybody willing to live on the outskirts of hell to help people is aces in his book.

"So I've deposited $6,000 in the Banco de Inglaterra in San Jose—$1,000 from Harold and the rest from me. We're not giving you this money, Jack, we're investing it. We expect to get it back and then some. I understand the need to keep this money out of sight from the Peace Corps. They've got their rules and I understand them, but you wouldn't be your mother's son if you didn't see the bigger picture. Be careful, buddy. You might find yourself on the outside looking in. I told Dwight about your idea of using the baseball league as your base of operations and he's agreed that we will send some more uniforms and gloves and stuff, and we'll send them through the Peace Corps office in

San Jose, so you can use baseball as both your base and your cover. Good luck, Jack. Tafah is out in the barn waiting for you, and so am I, most days."

Baseball at the Nicaraguan end of Costa Rica was not only popular; it was perpetual. The season started, as best as I could figure, on April first and wrapped up around the end of March. And using terms I learned in journalism school, it was a built-in marketing delivery system for the co-op. The players and the early-adapters of the co-op were one and the same.

Just as I had hoped, the managers of the various town teams were delighted with the added prestige of being the co-op representative, although prestige often preceded understanding.

One of my favorite managers was Carlos Ruiz from the near-by village of Canalete. He must have hounded his poor wife to keep his uniform cleaned and ironed, because it always looked like it had just come back from the cleaners. Carlos wore his uniform like old European town burghers wore their sashes—dignified and with formality. It did hurt his ability as a player, however, because he refused to slide. Sliding, like throwing at the opposing batter's head, was a big part of OTABCO baseball, and most of the players would slide just for the hell of it. Not Carlos. He'd even stare you down after a hard tag.

When Mayor Melba realized that the co-op was going to loan and collect money, she quickly opted out. Victor took her place, but laughingly refused my offer of an OTABCO jersey. "Doesn't really go with loafers," he explained. Mickey, however, was happy to manage the team and wear the shirt, so we were set.

Collette, John and I met often in San Jose to map out strategy, and meet with our banker. We'd sit at a back table at Oldimar's Bar Soda Palace, scribbling ideas, numbers, names and places. John proved a wizard on the business end. "We are going to need every member of the co-op to have a stake in the game," he said. "This is going to confuse the fuck out of people at first. They're going to think the co-op is a place to borrow money, and it will be eventually, but first it must be a place they stick some of their own dough, no matter how tiny. This will show them that they really are one of the owners, and that a rising tide will lift all their god-damned boats. Also it not only makes them part owners, it makes them all loan officers. If one of their neighbors is dragging his feet on repaying a loan, they will realize that it's them that's being stiffed, and they can suggest that he pay up by taking him out in the back yard and beating the living shit out of him."

"Did you learn your eloquence at Brown or did you just pick it up naturally at reform school?" I asked idly. "If we're ever asked to present our work plan to the ambassador, let me do the talking." I looked at Collette. "What do you think?"

"John's got a point. You can't play if you can't ante. And the thousand loan officers is a brilliant idea. But how much money can poor people put up?"

I took a thoughtful sip of my Los Gigantes milk shake (guava, Oldimar's invention). "Victor says he thinks twenty-five *colones* is about right. That's just shy of five bucks. I don't have a clue. I see people buying cigarettes three at a time because they can't afford a pack, so my money meter is broken. Victor says yes, but they *are* buying cigarettes, every single day. It's just a matter of priorities. He also said that he doesn't want to be just a figurehead boss of the co-op; he wants to be an investor. He said he'd invest twenty-five hundred *colones* if we will agree to use the money to give a double-your-money incentive to the first hundred members."

"Well, shit oh dear, that's perfect," John bellowed, pulling away from the table and rising to his full Kodiak bear size. "You two can stay here and diddle each other as much as you want. I'm going back to Golfito to sign up my first hundred members. *Hasta luego, amigos.* That means see you later, in case you're interested. I just might get the hang of this Spanish shit after all."

We watched him depart in silence. I smiled sheepishly and took Collette's hand. "And here I thought I was going out of my way to pretend you were just one of the guys. Busted, but at least it's John, our very own potty mouth poet laureate. I don't think anybody else has noticed."

Oldimar walked up with a rag slung over his arm and pretended to clean the table. "Don't want to break up the birds of love, but there's a man looking for you, Jack. Been here three times. Only gives his front name, but he talks cowboy like you. Maybe he's a friend? Know a man name of Larry?"

"Well, shit oh dear," I sighed.

* * *

The co-op proved an instant success and pain in the ass in equal measure. In less than a month, we had more than 100 members sprinkled among our three towns. But John, Collette and I were awash in bank deposits, receipts, contracts and loan applications. We were in over our heads and needed help.

I was at my usual corner table at the Bar Soda Palace, shuffling papers and writing down figures when I saw Oldimar lip-point toward the silhouette of a man standing between me and the setting sun.

"That's him," Oldimar stage-whispered, his cigarette bobbing in his mouth.

I knew immediately who it was, but in the two seconds it took him to approach, I must have debated a dozen times whether to stand up and greet him or bolt for the back door.

"Hey, Larry," I said with an insincerity that surprised me. Apparently parts of me were still making up their mind between flight or fight.

Two years ago I had last seen a young preppy Larry Reznick. A balding, middle-aged Larry Reznick sat down in the plastic chair next to me. "Hey, Jackson. Humphrey Bogart here said I'd run into you. Well, he called you the boy from Oklahoma, but I figured it was you. I've been coming in here for weeks." He smiled that famous Reznick smile. "I wasn't really stalking you. I just don't have anywhere else to go at the moment." He nervously lit a cigarette. "I'm sort of between jobs. And to tell you the truth, you may be my last best chance. I'm sort of running low on countries . . . and friends."

"I'm your friend, Larry, as long as I can afford it."

His smile sagged just a bit. "I don't really deserve that. Didn't I leave your car in perfect condition, with more than enough money in the glove compartment to cover all of your expenses?"

"Well, yes, but the glove compartment was in Guadalajara, along with the rest of the car. Plus you had just threatened to knee-cap me."

He raised his eyebrows like a kid and turned his head thoughtfully. "Um, yeah, there was that. But you know, bygones and boomer sooner and all that shit, okay?" He pointed to the big ledger with scraps of paper scattered about the table. "What's all that?"

"That is the rock I may have to push up the mountain for the rest of my life. A couple of friends and I have started a co-op, but it is turning into a paper blizzard. Keeping track of hundreds of accounts is impossible. Even if we make a profit, how am I going to distribute it? And what if we take a loss? Who loses? How much?"

Larry took the pencil from my hand and turned the ledger to him. "That's really no big deal, boy from Oklahoma. It's called unitization. You probably forgot that I was an accounting major, among others. Here, let's take a look at this."

Four hours later we had every entry up to date, every member assigned a unit value to his account and OTABCO had hired its first full-time employee—a chief financial officer named Larry Reznick.

CHAPTER 23

Victor found office space for Larry in San Jose upstairs in one of the family business coffee warehouses. It was a great space in addition to being free, and it smelled terrific. Collette and I would often have our breakfast there when we were in town, eating those flaky little crescent rolls that were never quite stale and never quite fresh, but good enough when you are in love.

The co-op was going well, but between it and Collette, I was neglecting the baseball league and the guys were starting to complain. So when a new shipment of baseball gear arrived at Peace Corps headquarters, I sent a telegram to Mickey asking him to get in touch with Carlos and a few other managers and set up an OTABCO baseball meeting. Then to solidify my co-op cover, I asked Frank Le Pommes to come with me to distribute the bats, gloves and balls. Flattered and a bit surprised by my sudden show of *bonhomie*, he readily agreed.

We arrived in the middle of the usual afternoon downpour, but with the help of Constantinopolis, Mickey and a few members of the *Osos* (that was the San Isidro team. It means Bears), we got the stuff into the storage shed before the cardboard boxes melted.

Frank was very impressed with Mickey's starched uniform with its military pleats and, of course, Conti's Oklahoma City Indians baseball cap, which the little guy wore every waking moment, and probably to bed.

We hung around Mickey's office drinking orange Fantas and talking baseball. Frank was amazed that Mickey's English was so good and peppered him with questions.

"What's the Spanish word for baseball?" he asked enthusiastically.

"You're going to love this, Frank, right, Mickey?" I said

"Yeah," Mickey laughed. "The words are spelled differently, but they sound the same. When I went into the merchant marines, the only thing I could understand in English was baseball. Here it's *Beisbol.* They call *bolas* and *estraics*, you hit with a *bate* and steal a *base,* maybe hit a *jonron.* The outfielders are called gardeners, though, *jardineros.*

"Wow," Frank said, turning to me. "Maybe I should send John McNaughton up here. He might actually get some work done."

"I'd be glad to have his help," I answered silkily, and was reminded once again why John and I couldn't stand that pile of seersucker pomposity.

Later we took the colorful ox cart across the bridge and into town, with the kids providing a running and laughing entourage. At the end of the bridge was a handmade banner that said "Welcome Peace Corps to First OTABCO League Tournament." Mickey had been busy. And when we got to the soccer field, it wasn't a soccer field anymore. There was no skinned infield, but they'd made a pitcher's mound and somebody, I suspected Victor, had even found bags of lime which the men were using to line the field. It looked like a real baseball field, and Frank was impressed.

"Well, Harjo, I like what you've done here. This is Peace Corps at its best. Congratulations. Do you play?"

"No, Frank, it wouldn't be fair. These guys are still learning the game. So I'm the umpire and settle all disputes, which you will see are loud and often." I laughed. "Besides, when I step up to the plate, it's not baseball anymore. It's target practice. I've got the bruises to prove it."

I kept Frank so busy with baseball, he never asked me about the co-op. And I could tell by his wilting shirt collar that he didn't really want to ask me about anything. Like Mrs. James before him, he just wanted to get the hell out of there. Frank watched a couple of innings, got another of her seemingly endless supply of proclamations from Mayor Melba, then scurried back with Conti to catch the return flight to San Jose. Mickey had to excuse himself for a while, too, as he turned into air traffic control. But he was replaced by Victor, who once again had found a way to keep his loafers spotless.

After the game Victor and I stood behind the soccer net we had used as a backstop, watching some of the men barbequing a pig and passing around a bottle of the local moonshine, the ubiquitous ever-clear *guaro*, that could, and perhaps did, peel paint.

"Did you notice those guys watching the game from the bamboo behind right field?" he asked idly.

"Yeah, I didn't recognize them, though. I thought they must have been a team from another town, scouting the *Osos*."

"In a way they were. They asked me to invite you and the team to play them in baseball in Nicaragua." When I showed surprise, he said, "Don't worry. It's not that far. We can get there by boat in a few hours. They've got a real baseball field up there, with real bases and everything. And I think you might find their manager a very interesting guy."

"How so?"

"He's my old friend from Argentina—Che Guevara."

* * *

On Sunday a week later, I took some of my best players, plus Victor, Mickey and Carlos to this same cluster of buildings I'm living in now. Casimiro was there then as always, but everything else was different—bustling, full of life, and sure enough, with a real baseball field as good as any I had played in my American Legion days.

On the boat ride across a corner of Lake Nicaragua and up one of the dozens of tributaries that fed into it, I was surprised by Victor's ability to find the mouth of the river in what looked like one continuous jungle thicket to me. I also noticed that he had traded his city garb for jungle boots and chinos. "I've got about a million questions for you, Victor, but I'll start by asking how you find your way through this labyrinth. I'd be lost forever."

"I've been here many times and that is very much the idea. That bastard Somoza can't find the camp either, not that he knows there even is one." He laughed into the wind stirred by the motorboat. "And when he finally finds out, it will be too late."

"What do you mean 'too late'? Is Che Guevara planning an overthrow of Nicaragua?" I was incredulous.

"Let's just say that if this boat had a name, it would be 'Gramma'. No, just as he learned in Cuba, El Che won't have to overthrow anything. The Nicaraguan people will rise up and revolt against the bloody and corrupt Somoza regime. The people of Nicaragua are the kindling; El Che is just the match."

"Be careful, Victor. You play a dangerous game. If you knew your American history, you'd know that's exactly what John Brown said at Harper's Ferry about the slaves a hundred years ago, just before the Civil War. They didn't lift a finger to help him, couldn't really, and he was hanged. It doesn't always work the way you planned." Knowing what a true believer Victor was, I didn't have the heart to mention that the "match to the kindling" argument was also used by anti-Castro revolutionaries at the Bay of Pigs only the year before, a misadventure that got every single one of them killed. I just looked off into the distance. "Gramma?"

"Maybe you need a lesson in Cuban history, my friend. That was the name of the boat Castro and Che and their little band used to get from Mexico to Cuba. Sometimes things go precisely as planned. Fidel and Che took down Batista with 70 men, Jack, 70." He pointed to a break in the river undergrowth. "Get ready, we're almost here."

We approached a landing that seemed abandoned until four men with rifles and bandoleers appeared out of nowhere. I was startled, but two of my ball players started laughing and shouting greetings.

"Those are the Fonseca brothers," Victor said. "They used to work the cacao trees around San Isidro. You can bet the big one is on the baseball team. Talk about your *jonron.* He hits it a mile, just like Marvin Throneberry."

Casimiro ran up to grab my bag of baseballs, bats and gloves, and scurried away in the direction I assumed was the baseball field. We entered the camp like conquering heroes. Victor seemed to know everybody and was quickly engulfed in *abrazos,* victory yips and even an occasional salute as we slowly made our way to the schoolhouse.

The compound was alive with activity. Some men were working on the engine of an old Dodge Power Wagon quarter-ton, another group was putting a jeep back together and off to the left of the school was a boat yard with about a dozen of those long, narrow boats designed for river traffic. Outboard motors in various states of repair were scattered about the yard and everywhere was the smell of gasoline.

As we got close to the open-air school, I was surprised to see that a class was in session. Earnest young men with their ball point pens and what I now think of as my blue books were furiously copying notes from a blackboard that the teacher, in beard and bandoleers, tapped from time to time.

"I've got to say that surprises me, Victor. Student soldiers? What is this, West Point Nicaragua-style?"

"Maybe someday," Victor said, "but first we must teach them to read and write. Ignorant people can lead revolutions, my friend, but they can't lead countries. That was a hard lesson for Che to learn in Cuba, and became a sticking point between him and Fidel. Castro has a high tolerance for ignorance, and I must say corruption, if they are coupled with loyalty. Che will tell you that a dog can be loyal, but not president. Fidel will tell you what does it matter, he intends to be president forever. That is the difference between the two men—Che thinks in decades; Fidel thinks in hours. It is time you met our leader. He's in the infirmary, as usual."

"Is he ill?"

"No, Jack, he's a doctor. We all have our jobs to do. Come on."

While the rest of our men wandered off to the baseball field, Victor, Mickey and I walked to the tidy, screened-in infirmary. Che Guevara was seated next to a cot, wrapping the hand of a young man who regarded him with a combination of fear and adoration, a look I was to see often in Che's men.

Che leaned back and pulled the cigar out of his mouth. "Next time don't use a machete for a screw driver, okay, Juanito?" Like a lot of things I'd seen in the jungle, Che's voice was three sizes larger than his body. He was, in fact, slight with a scraggly beard that made him look almost boyish, and with the burning ember eyes of a night animal.

"Welcome, Victor. Is this the American you lured here so we could ransom him? How much do you think he will bring?" Seeing me stiffen, Che couldn't stifle one of those wheezing laughs that I learned were his asthmatic trademark.

"I couldn't find a rich one. This one sadly is a Peace Corps person with a value of maybe thirty dollars; maybe less. Hardly seems worth the effort, heh? But he does play baseball, and he comes from the same place as Mickey Mantle. Meet Jack Harjo from Oklahoma."

"Arshow, Arshow. Are you Indian? How do you do."

I looked at Victor in astonishment, then back to Guevara. "Yes I am, but how could you possibly know that?"

He gave another wet laugh. "I am a student of the cowboys and Indians. Arshow doesn't sound *gringo*". He returned his cigar to his mouth. "Back home, I was the only one in the movies who rooted for the Indians. And I read that half of Oklahoma is Indians. I took the chance. I hope to visit there someday. Maybe you will be my guide. Do you know Mickey Mantle? I think he, too, is Indian, no?"

"So they say, but I am afraid our comparison ends there. You will see when we play baseball."

Victor put his arm around my shoulder. "He has something better, *jefe*. Jack is the one I told you about with the wonderful idea about a co-op for the *campesinos* so they can borrow money, get paid fair prices for their beans and cacao and work together to take control of their lives."

"Ha. I think maybe soon we will turn all of Nicaragua into a co-op. It is a very good idea, Jack. May I call you Jack? Arshow is very hard for me." Before I could answer, he turned and pointed his cigar at Victor, coughing up another small laugh. "And don't forget the idea of bringing me someone to ransom. We are running out of money as usual, and we have no co-op yet. But Victor, next time bring me a rich one instead of a smart one."

CHAPTER 24

"You played baseball with fucking Che Guevara?" John shouted gleefully. "You must have balls of solid brass. Revolutionaries aren't known to dick around."

"Seriously, John," I said with as much gravitas as my semi-stoned state would allow. "I think you must have contracted tourniquet syndrome, or whatever you call it."

"It's called Tourette's syndrome, dumbass, and no I don't have it. Those poor fuckers spout dirty words when they don't mean to; every one of my dirty words is carefully plotted out in advance. I am the sultan of scatology; the Oracle of the Obscene. This is some righteous shit by the way, Larry."

"It ought to be. It's from my private blend of Panama Red and Managua Mountain Dew, both I am proud to say are trademarked and copyrighted by yours truly." He took the joint from John and offered it to me. "Want another hit?"

"No thanks, I'm as stoned as I want to be," I said, offering silent homage (35) to Mickey Mantle. "What do you mean, 'trademarked and copyrighted'?"

Larry, John and I were sitting out on John's screened-in front porch of his little *casita* among the banana trees in Golfito. Golfito looked like an abandoned set to some tropical movie now that American Fruit had left town. The neat little company-town houses with their identical screened-in porches sat half-empty, waiting for the government jobs that never materialized, the beach hotel that would never be built and the technical school that was still on the drawing boards in San Jose.

John had set up a chance for me to speak with the banana growers about the co-op, and even though my Spanish was far from perfect, it was light-years ahead of John's. Perhaps because the growers were now pretty much on their own, they got the idea of the co-op almost immediately, and we signed up 14 new members in a single day. It had been hard work for all three of us and we were sitting on John's porch listening to the night birds and drinking rum and cokes when Larry produced a half-cigarette, half-cigar that he called gage, which is the hip musician's word for marijuana.

I never thought about marijuana one way or the other back in Oklahoma. Like every other college student, I guess, I tried it a few times, but I didn't have much use for it. Judy liked to smoke it before we had sex, which actually made me slightly resentful. I wondered if she needed the joint to enjoy sex with me, and when I found out the answer was basically yes, I turned away from both of them. And then Larry's little Texas dust-up not only cost me a lot of grief, it almost cost me a few months in a leg cast again. Besides, I was just beginning to really like *Flor de Caña*. But I was intrigued at how casual both John and Larry were about it.

"You bet your ass," Larry said, holding the half-smoked joint in the air. "This little beauty holds the key to my fortune in its little stoned hands, if I may mix my metaphors."

"You may," John said with Victorian dignity. "Don't think for a minute I'm going to forget about What's-His-Face, but I, too, am piqued. How do you trademark grass?"

"Not the actual commodity itself, my dung-tongued friend, but its packaging. You may not know this, but I have it on deep and reliable authority that now that Kennedy is president, marijuana will soon be legalized. How can it be otherwise?" Larry pointed to the bottle of rum. "It's better for you than alcohol and tobacco, and if it brings in half the tax revenue that booze and cigarettes do, there won't be any income tax anymore. Grass is going to stimulate the economy, the music industry, the appetite, both sexual and otherwise, it'll create thousands of jobs, we'll have grass stores right next to liquor stores . . ."

"Not to mention world peace," John said. "Who would want to go to war when ice cream tastes so fucking good, not to mention yogurt, blueberry buckle and glazed donuts. Really good idea, and about time, but what does that have to do with you?"

"Among my many near-majors, I was all over pre-law, and it dawned on me one night that if and when marijuana was legalized, it would be lights out for the right guy. Grass would leave the domain of home-grown shit sold in alleys by long-haired freaks with bad teeth and body odor, and enter corporate board rooms. The tobacco industry will be falling all over itself to market and sell grass the way it sells Winstons and Camels. It will be a billion-dollar industry. So I got out my textbooks on trademarks and copyrights and went to work."

Larry stood up and walked to the hammock that served as John's day bed. He slid effortlessly into the hammock and with his finger began to conduct a silent symphony. "I now own American and international trademarks on, let's see, Acapulco Gold, Maui Wowie, Panama Red, Kona Blue, Managua Mountain Dew, Santa Barbara Giggle Grass and Sinsemilla. Liggett and Myers will be beating a path to my door, if the American Tobacco Company isn't there first."

I was having a hard time following the conversation. Every time Larry mentioned a name, I'd see the color. "If you are right, it looks like you'll be in the chips, whatever that means," I said. "But I don't know. You couldn't get a legal drink in Oklahoma until 1957." I giggled. "People had to drink in alleys with freaks with bad teeth and B.O. It can take a long time to turn some folks around." I fell back on an argument I'd heard at the newspaper. "Besides, it may not be as harmless as you think. Would you really want to fly in an airplane with a pilot who is stoned?"

"That is so bullshit," John said. "I wouldn't want to fly in an airplane with a pilot who is drunk, either, but that doesn't keep us from selling liquor in every saloon, restaurant and grocery store in the country. And I bet you Che Fucking Guevara wishes he had thought of it first. He wouldn't have to overthrow Nicaragua; he could just buy the god-damned place. So now that I've heard your marketing plan, I want in. How much for ten percent? I'll even pay you in glazed donuts."

* * *

The co-op went absolutely gang-busters. Everything just seemed to fall into place. By Thanksgiving (a holiday that befuddled Costa Ricans almost as much as Halloween) we had more than two hundred members. We made our first loans to three of Collette's women's circles for sewing machines. In a very short time the money was completely paid back with five percent interest. This was slightly higher than banks, but John said he had learned in economics that it was access to money, not interest rates, that would drive the co-op. Besides, it was a moot point, he said. There wasn't a bank in the world that would loan our people "a fucking penny." He was absolutely right.

I began sending lengthy letters home to Daddy and Mr. James, which I considered my report to investors. I told them all about marketing, interest rates and unitization, how many members we had, and some of our loans (in addition to the sewing machines, we had financed the purchase of a cow in San Isidro and the purchase of six casitas in Golfito which were being turned into rentals, with a priority to co-op members).

I guess Daddy had lived in and around newspapers for so many years, he showed the letters to Art Triester at the *Ardmorite.* Art saw the human interest and local investor angle immediately. He took a couple of my chatty letters and turned them into a front-page story that went more than a thousand words. Mr. James was quoted, saying he'd seen for himself the desperate need of "those brave pioneers of the jungle," and applauded my efforts to apply good old American business know-how to third world problems.

Art's headline ran four columns: "Oklahoma Peace Corpsman's Plan For Prosperity: Banking and Baseball." When I read the article, I couldn't help chuckling about what my mother would have made of such a saccharine (78) headline. Art was still writing like Pepper Holiday.

A couple of weeks later I got a telegram to meet "as soon as possible" with Frank Le Pommes at Peace Corps headquarters in San Jose.

Frank paced the floor of his office, looking at every object in the room except me. "Well, Jackson, old man, it looks like you're a hero. Apparently an article about you and that co-op thing showed up in your hometown newspaper. I'd like to remind you that clearing a story like that with me beforehand would be common courtesy, if not precisely written policy." He puffed out a breath and looked skyward, which was about as exasperated as his Back Bay upbringing would allow. "Nevertheless, even though I didn't see the article, Peace Corps Washington did, including the Old Man himself. They love it, and think the story could go a long way to counteract some of the less-favorable volunteer stories coming out of Africa. *Newsweek* magazine agreed that it would make a holiday feel-good story, and it's sending a reporter down here next week to interview you. Good for you, and all that. But let me remind you that the co-op story simply cannot be about you; it's got to be about the local people. It's their show, Harjo, you are just there to help. Now I know you know your way around journalists, so shape this story so it's not about you. You got that?"

"Absolutely, sir," I replied loudly and sincerely.

Three days later as Collette and I waited at the airport in Limon for the reporter, I suddenly realized how difficult that promise was going to be to keep. Stepping off the plane with camera and notebook in hand was the *Newsweek* reporter, a red nimbus-haired beauty better known to me as Judy Wickerman.

CHAPTER 25

The terminal at Limon airport was one of those brightly-painted cinder block and corrugated tin roof modern monstrosities designed by architects who wouldn't be caught dead in one. This one had an inexplicable gap of three feet between the roof and top of the wall. The thought was, I guess, to make the building airy and cheerful by creating a natural breezeway. But at least in the case of Limon, it let in every bird, lizard and flying insect, not to mention the occasional monkey and bat.

The resident iguana sunned himself on the wall overlooking the baggage claim, bobbing his head in satisfaction over the American sports fishermen who had come to catch tarpon and bonita, get drunk and get laid, not necessarily in that order.

Collette saw Judy at the top of the ramp, then shot me a quizzical look and a "what are you waiting for?" toss of the head towards the plane.

I was struck both stupid and paralyzed. I just stared wide-eyed at Collette and shook my head no, silently pleading for forgiveness for the bundle of lies and half-truths I felt were sure to follow. Collette caught on immediately, of course, as any woman would, squinted her eyes into death rays, then did an about-face and, throwing both arms in the air, shouted "Welcome to Costa Rica, Judy. What a pleasant surprise."

Like a guilty child looking for mitigation, I drew some satisfaction from Collette's own little white lie of enthusiasm. Collette, and most of the girls in training for that matter, didn't like Judy much, especially after she pasted herself against Victor and started acting like the dragon guarding the box of gold.

Judy gave Collette the obligatory hug and air kiss, then slung her camera case over one shoulder and military-marched up to me with eyes that danced in anticipation. Then Judy thoroughly perplexed me by looking over, around and finally through me. It was instantly clear that whatever reason Judy had for coming to Costa Rica, it wasn't to rekindle our relationship. I was both relieved and annoyed by this. She stuck out her hand and gave me the same no-nonsense wooden handshake she had given when she dusted me off six months earlier.

"Hello, Jack. How very good to see you. Congratulations are in order. My editors think your co-op will make a great holiday story." She turned her head slightly to Collette. "What do you say we repair to that little café inside the terminal? Victor wired me to say he'd pick us up there." She suddenly turned coquettish. "Is he here yet? I can't wait to see him."

Judy hadn't noticed that I had yet to utter a word. Finally I croaked, "Victor? Repair?"

In that school-marmish way I had seen so often in the past, Judy led us by the hand into the open-air alcove of little plastic tables and little plastic chairs. When the waitress came to the table, Judy ordered three Cokes in talk-to-your-maid Spanish without even looking our way for agreement. I guess Collette and I should have been offended, but Judy was so obviously, and naturally, in charge we just sat there with our mouths agape.

When the Cokes arrived, Judy placed a straw in each one, wrapped them in a paper serviette, and passed them out like favors at a birthday party. "Victor should be here any minute, guys. He said the road between here and San Jose isn't all that wonderful, but he figured we'd need his Toyota while we're here." She placed both of her hands over Collette's and bent forward like a schoolgirl. "And congratulations to you, too, Collette. How wonderful. I can see it in your eyes. You and Jack are lovers, which pleases me very much. It takes one to know one, I guess."

Collette roared with laughter and patted Judy's hands. "For god's sake, girl, do you ever inhale? Yes, I'm very much in love with Jack, but the question is, how the hell did you know?"

"Victor and I have been in constant contact ever since they kicked me out of the Peace Corps." Judy's eyes flicked toward me. "Yep, Jack, kicked out. I whitewashed it a little when you and I last met. Didn't want to hurt your feelings, I guess, and I was kind of shell-shocked. It's not every day you get caught *in flagrante* in the school cafeteria." To her credit, she giggled.

"Looks like you landed on your feet," I said uncomfortably, and immediately wished I'd selected another metaphor. "*Newsweek* is a very big deal. How did you pull it off? You never seemed that interested in journalism when I was doing it."

She tossed her auburn mane. "Now don't get testy, Jack. Of course I was interested, just busy doing other things. Then suddenly I got very unbusy. I needed a job, bad, and I was damaged goods. So I decided to eat a little Wickerman doo-doo and cash in on being a congressman's daughter. I went to my father, God forgive me, and told him the Peace Corps was just too liberal for me, and I needed a job. A week later I'm a stringer for *Newsweek's* Washington bureau. But just a stringer, which means I get paid by the piece. In the newsroom they call it 'eat what you kill.' I'm very much on probation, but they did give me these prestigious business cards." She laughed, pulled two cards out of her purse and dealt one to each of us: Judy Wickerman, *Newsweek,* 1085 Farragut Square, Washington 23, District of Columbia.

"I was in my father's office one morning and when I saw that piece they did on you in the *Ardmorite*, Jack, I could hardly believe it. It's a good story. But it's also a ticket to ride. I pitched it to my editors, told them I knew you well, and they bought it. So here I am with a plane ticket and an expense account. If they like it, the story runs the week between Christmas and New Year."

"And if they don't like it?" I muttered to the card.

Judy giggled again and patted the camera bag. "Oh, they'll like it, just so long as I get some good pictures and you promise to, um, polish the story up a bit. Will you, Jack?" She didn't wait for the answer, just leapt to her feet. "Look guys, here comes Victor. Jesus, is he good looking."

I long ago noticed that Victor had mastered the art of the late entrance, and he didn't disappoint this time. He literally ran across the airport, arms akimbo, grabbed Judy in a wrestler's embrace and swung her in circles, shouting "*Ay, mi amor, mi querida, mi vida.*" No translation necessary, right?

As Judy and Victor spun in their lovers' dance, Collette patted my hand. "Do we look like that to other people? No wonder everybody and their pet monkey knows we're lovers. Let's get them to the women's sewing club before they start doing it on one of these tables."

We drove over pot-holed cobblestone torture streets to one of the poorest *barrios* in Limon. Victor and Judy were comfortably ensconced in the front seats, Judy snapping photos of everything, while Collette and I bounced around the back like billiard balls in a boxcar. "And to think we could have ridden mules and saved our kidneys," I said. "This article better be good."

Collette laughed above the noise of the struggling jeep. "I think that's going to depend on how much you polish it, Jack. Judy's down here to fuck Victor. Everything else is a distant second." She looked over my shoulder into the front seat. "Can't say I blame her. He is a handsome devil."

We arrived at a thatched-roof open-air building that had been an auto repair shop before the owner vanished earlier in the year, taking his meager inventory of cars and car parts with him. The well-oiled and hard-packed dirt floor had a pleasant smell that reminded me of country roads in Oklahoma. The three long work tables had two sewing machines in the middle of each, with bolts of cloth at one end. If a place with a dirt floor could be called spotless, this little sewing factory was spotless.

A sturdy-looking black woman engulfed Collette in a fleshy embrace and led us to the center table where plates had been set out with fat tamales wrapped in banana leaves, fried *platanos*, chunks of goat cheese and sausages, hearts of palm, saltine crackers and cookies. Large pitchers of fruit punch and paper cups were lined up along the back of the table, with a woman standing at parade rest behind each one, dressed uncomfortably in starched dresses that previously had only seen the light of day at Sunday mass.

The large woman, who everybody called doña Esperanza out of respect for her clear leadership role, took Collette in one hand and Judy in the other, talking non-stop as she handed us little plates of this and that.

Judy was out of her element and shot Collette a look. "Do I dare eat this?" she whispered.

"It's up to you, of course," Collette said gaily as if she was discussing the weather. "But it did cost these women almost a week's profit, they worked all morning to prepare it, and if you don't eat something, I'll strangle you with my bare hands. Try the hearts of palm."

Victor took a big bite out of one of the over-sized tamales and started laying down a barrage of compliments that turned Esperanza into a giggling school girl. "Get a photo of us, Judy. The more pictures you shoot, the less you'll have to eat."

"And get some shots of the sewing machines, okay?" I had awakened from my self-imposed somnambulance (83) to finally join the party. "Those represent the first loans the co-op ever made."

The place took on a festive atmosphere, with the beefy Esperanza dragging one shy woman after another in front of Judy to display the baby clothes and rough work pants that were the stock and trade of the co-op. Victor pulled out a wad of money and made a theatrical purchase of a little dress from one of the proud and solemn women, with Judy's expensive Leica clicking away. I had to admit Judy looked very competent with the camera.

After an hour or so, Victor gave a moving speech to the women about their pioneering efforts with the co-op, how proud his country was of them, how they would lead the way for women all over the world and flattered doña Esperanza until the poor woman almost swooned. Was I looking at the future president of Costa Rica? He said he was damaged beyond repair, but there was that look in his eye.

Back in the land cruiser, Collette gave Judy the names of all the women, although I knew the editors would never use them, and was bubbling over with pride. "This really has a chance," she said. "This co-op idea really has a chance, not just here in Limon." She reached into the front seat and took Judy's hand in the first gesture of real affection toward her I had seen from my street-savvy girlfriend. "Judy, with your help we can get this story out to Peace Corps volunteers in every nook and cranny of the globe—Peru, Ethiopia, hell, Tierra del Fuego. We can make a difference, Judy. We really can."

Judy got swept up in the enthusiasm. "I'll try my best, Collette. With Jack's help, I'm going to write a piece that will knock my editor's socks off." She turned her head to me. "Now we need to get to, where is it, San Isidro to meet your farmers and baseball players, Jack. Great pictures there, too, I'll bet."

Victor laughed. "Don't take too many pictures of guys standing around the outfield. You may get the surprise of your life."

Judy looked curiously at Victor. "Surprised how?"

I was a little miffed at being shunted to the sidelines again, I guess. "He probably means Che Guevara. He's come to a few of the games," I lied off-handedly.

Judy pulled her hand away from Collette and grabbed Victor's arm. "Che Guevara is in San Isidro?"

Victor laughed again. "No, but close enough. He's in Nicaragua now and then. Like to meet him?"

"Oh my God, Victor. No American journalist has interviewed him since the early days of the revolution. I thought he was in the Congo. This could make my career, darling. I know you said you knew him, but I thought that was long ago. Can you get me an interview? He's in Nicaragua? Where in Nicaragua?"

"A mere two hours from our baseball field by dugout canoe," I said, sounding smug even to myself.

CHAPTER 26

I have to admit Judy did a good job of reporting the co-op. At my suggestion, she asked Frank to accompany her to Golfito, where she took pictures of Frank and John McNaughton standing among the banana trees, pretending to like each other. When she found out that Larry Reznick was working the main co-op office in San Jose, she was delighted and spent an entire day with him, snapping pictures and learning the financial aspects of the business . . . a reunion that in retrospect I should have looked into a little more closely.

Judy was observant and took good notes, which is really half the battle in reporting, especially with a magazine like *Newsweek*, where a barrage of editors would rewrite everything anyway. This was lucky, because her mind had already started to drift to what she considered the big picture, just as it had during her days of sit-ins and marches.

When she and Victor arrived in San Isidro, Mickey and I had prepared the obligatory baseball game, which really only interested Judy in its potential to draw out Che Guevara. It was all she could talk about. "Do you think he will come, darling?" she asked Victor. For some reason, her use of the word "darling" was annoying, maybe because she had never used that term with me. I didn't love her anymore, but I could still dredge up resentment.

Judy became obsessed with the idea of meeting and interviewing Che Guevara. Sitting in Mickey's LACSA office as we waited for the morning plane from San Jose, she tugged insistently on Victor's sleeve. "Don't you see? This is my career moment. He's never been interviewed by an American journalist before. Did I say that already? I'm very excited. This co-op article," she waved back-handed toward me once, like she was shooing a fly, "brought me to Costa Rica, but interviewing Guevara would keep me here in your arms for months. We must seize the moment, my darling." Did I see Victor roll his eyes, or was I just projecting? In any case, he obliged, and changed my life forever.

* * *

The *Newsweek* article came out December 28, 1962, with me on the cover, wearing an OTABCO baseball cap and pointing at some numbers on a bank ledger book being worked on by Mickey. The cover cutline said "The Peace Corps in Latin America: *Buenos Dias* to Baseball and Banking." Inside were the picture of Frank and John, which delighted Frank, and one of Collette and Esperanza hovering over the sewing machines, plus one of me signaling safe as Carlos pretended to slide into home. Because of recent negative publicity in Ethiopia, Peace Corps Washington was as happy as Frank. We even got a personal letter from Sargent Shriver. Although we didn't plan it, Collette being black, John white and me both a cowboy and an Indian played right into the "melting pot America" story line, and we got coverage on Dave Garroway and Paul Harvey. WKY-TV even interviewed Mr. James as the provider of the uniforms, complete with some pictures I shot when Mister and Mrs. James had come to San Isidro. Daddy was asked to go on TV, too, but he declined, gently but firmly.

The international edition of *Newsweek* didn't carry the same cover as the state-side edition, which was common, so I was able to avoid the cover-boy publicity in Costa Rica at least. Ardmore, on the other hand, went nuts. I was the first Oklahoman since Pretty Boy Floyd to make the cover of a national magazine, and that was the *Police Gazette*. Come to think of it, old Chock Floyd and I had a lot in common, being part Indian and criminals and everything. Art Triester got *Newsweek* to cough up some of Judy's pictures of me pretending to do various co-op things, always in my OTABCO cap, that made page one of the *Ardmorite* New Year's Day 1963.

Then, just like my "waiting for a hamburger" story, the co-op story disappeared, replaced by news of the Mona Lisa coming to America and the Beatles exploding all over the world. Collette and I escaped to our favorite rendezvous in Puntarenas, where Oldimar's old friend Celso had gotten hold of some Beatles' records from one of the cruise ships. Collette and I sat listening to "Please, Please Me" in perplexed silence. Finally Collette looked down at her plate. "Where in the hell is Little Richard when you need him?" she asked nobody. "It's times like this when I think we didn't just leave the United States; I feel like we left earth." She waved a fried shrimp menacingly at me. "And my friend, I keep hearing how much Judy wants to meet Che Guevara. Can you and Victor please get her to Nicaragua or wherever the hell he is . . . and leave her there?"

* * *

It didn't take long. January was a wet, slow time for the cacao cutters, money was running out because it was just before the dry season, and my guys on the baseball team were itching for a chance to play ball and drink a little Nicaraguan rum. And Che, it seemed, was just as interested in meeting the woman my guys called *La Rosada* (the Pink Lady) as she was to meet him.

Judy cut quite a figure, putting herself out as Guevara bait. She was the only woman in San Isidro, maybe all of Costa Rica, who wore pants. She knew it and she flaunted it. Victor got her a horse from his coffee *finca*, and the two of them danced their way through the rubber trees and high-canopied jungles like characters out of an Errol Flynn movie. She learned to shoot a rifle, taking down oranges and other jungle fruits in target practice with deadly accuracy. The young men who worked as cacao cutters (there were no old cacao cutters) were stunned into lustful silence. Judy was starring in her own movie, and loving it.

Then one day Victor said the meeting and the baseball game were all set. He warned Judy that she could come, but she would have to leave her camera and notebook behind. She grabbed one of my OTABCO baseball caps and mushed it down on her wild red hair. "I understand, my love, it's just baseball and how do you do this time. Please tell me he speaks English. My Spanish is abysmal."

Victor smiled. "He does, but he may not. It depends on how much he trusts you. But he will understand every word you say. Besides, I will be at your side every minute. And remember, just because you will meet him in a Nicaraguan jungle doesn't mean he's a *campesino*. He's sophisticated and highly informed, a medical doctor and a true leader. You will fall under his spell." He laughed. "Just don't fall too far."

We arrived at Che's camp one Sunday around noon. If anything the place was even busier than the last time I was there, with men filling rucksacks with rain gear, pans, canteens and small bags of rice.

As we walked back to the infirmary that doubled as Che's office, I turned to Victor. "Looks like they're getting ready to move out. Planning a trip?"

"Maybe just a little one," Victor said quietly. "Anyway it's better to be ready. Sometimes you go for a visit. Sometimes the visitors come to you."

Judy swept her arm dramatically in an arc over her head. "This is exactly how I imagined a guerrilla camp would look," she said. "I'd give a thousand dollars for my camera right now." She grabbed Victor's arm excitedly. "This is it, Victor, I can feel it. I'm going to write a book about Che's victory against that evil dictator Somoza. You are going to do it, Victor; you are going to bring freedom to Nicaragua, then Guatemala, then all of Central America."

We heard the familiar coughing laugh behind us.

"Why stop there?" Che asked in Spanish. "What about Mexico? Jamaica? I like Jamaica. Their cigars are almost as good as Cuban." He pulled the cigar from his mouth and pointed it at Judy. "So you are the Pink Lady my men talk about. Welcome, Pink Lady, you are in your home here. Ah, and Mister Jack, you, too, welcome." He pulled out a copy of the American version of *Newsweek* with my face plastered all over the cover. "Congratulations, Jack. Your co-ops sound like a very good idea. Maybe when we take over Nicaragua, I will make you my minister of banking."

Judy understood just enough to try to take control of the conversation. "What about me?" she said in English. "I wrote the article. And I'm going to write the book that will make you even more famous than you are now. Maybe you could make me minister of propaganda or something."

Che and Victor just stood in amused silence, with Che pulling thoughtfully on his cigar.

After about two beats, Judy laughed, too. "Got another one of those cigars, Doctor Guevara?"

"I like your Pink Lady, Victor. Very much."

CHAPTER 27

Over the next few months Victor and Judy spent more and more time in Nicaragua. She was living with Victor at the coffee plantation and had completely gained the trust of Guevara and his men. She traded her OTABCO baseball cap for a beret like Che's, and had her run of the camp. On one of my baseball visits, I saw her at the infirmary with a rifle hoisted on one knee and smoking a cigar like Bonnie without her Clyde.

I didn't have a lot of time to think about it, because suddenly the co-op was very busy, thanks to John McNaughton. I had forgotten what a savvy businessman John was under that profane bluster. And if I had forgotten, the buyers from the American Fruit Company were completely unaware, and never knew what hit them.

For months OTABCO had been buying banana futures from the growers and paying fair prices. By the time the American Fruit buyers came to Golfito, we owned more than 70 percent of the banana crop. American Fruit needed that harvest to meet its European obligations. In the old days they'd pick the growers off one at a time—getting them drunk and then paying ten cents on the dollar. But this time the buyers found themselves in bare-knuckle negotiations with John. John had been busy, getting letters of inquiry from Dole in Panama, just enough to prove we were willing to look elsewhere. In language that would have made the Teamsters proud, John told the buyers that we had the money to sit on this year's crop rather than sell it at their prices. He may have said something about bananas and putting them where the sun doesn't shine, or words to that effect. The buyers, who probably weren't the American Fruit first team to begin with and had little experience at real negotiations, doubled their offer and then doubled it again before John took his foot off their throat. American Fruit still made plenty of money, but so did we.

Did we ever. We were awash in money in fact. Larry came down to Golfito from San Jose and showed us where we could provide a modest bonus to the banana co-op members, build an ample reserve and still pay a respectable dividend to our investors. It felt really good to send Daddy a check for $500, a payment I imagine he never expected. Even Mr. James got $100, and I got boxes of baseball equipment in return.

Larry brought the growers' bonuses, all cash, in two soccer bags he bought at the open-air market in San Jose. When I expressed concern about carrying so much money, Larry just patted his right side under his guayabera shirt. "Don't worry, partner," he said in his best gravelly Ralph Meeker imitation, "I'm packing heat. Little something I learned from my drug-running days in Panama. You have to understand. Everything is done in cash down here. These guys don't have bank accounts. You need an ID to cash a check. Think they have any? And we aren't going to get all Calvinist about how they spend their dough, either. We're going to give them money, and they are going to spend it, some wisely, some not. But now, at least they're only going to blow their bonus, not a full year's pay."

Victor took his dividend and immediately converted it to a pile of Nicaraguan *cordobas* as thick as a brick and handed it to Guevara, which got El Che's attention big time.

* * *

A few days later Victor asked me to come with him to meet with Che. We took Victor's small outboard that got us there in half the time my baseball team had to endure. We walked past the ever-busy boat house and repair shop, classrooms and weapons depot to Che's clinic cum office. Standing next to Che was Judy, her red hair taking on Medusa-like tangles that made her look kind of scary. Well, that, plus the bandoleer slung across her chest. She looked like the poster girl for *La Revolución.*

Che waved me over to his cluttered table. He pulled his cigar from his mouth and smiled. "I'm proud of you, Jack. I hear that you and your *cooperativa* stuck a knife into the fat bellies of the American Fruit imperialists. It seems we are working the same streets now, true?"

I sat down stiffly. "Don't get me wrong, please," I said, cutting my eyes toward Judy. *Could this possibly be the same woman I went to protect in New Orleans?* "I am not at war with the American Fruit Company. We wanted a fair price for our growers and got it. But the buyers got a good deal, too. Everybody got happy. Including, according to our friend Victor, yourself, don Che."

He smiled again. "It's true. Victor shared his portion of the payments with all of us here at camp. It is rare that my men see real money these days. That is what I want to talk to you about." His voice grew softer and he leaned across the table with those wide, innocent eyes pleading for understanding.

"I once told you that your co-op would be the model for all of Nicaragua when the people get rid of that frog Somoza. True, but we will never rid ourselves of The Frog unless we have funds. Revolutions that spring from the people in the fields don't need much money, but they need some. And this revolution needs a little more than others, I am afraid. Revolutions need revolutionaries." He pointed to the very school rooms that now make up my home away from home. "See those classes? We are growing revolutionaries here quickly, like tomatoes in a greenhouse. Fully-developed, literate, committed local leaders who will hold this beautiful country together when we move on to other oppressed nations like Honduras and Bolivia. When these brave young men stand ready to lead, the people will support them. That is exactly what happened when Fidel and I freed Cuba from the corrupt government of Batista. But Fidel was native Cuban. The people adored him as their favorite son. Food and lodging were always free. Nicaragua is different, at least for now, and Jack, bullets cost money wherever you are, and so do rifles."

Judy switched the conversation to English with hardly anyone noticing. "Make us part of your co-op, Jack. Put us in as investment partners. Many of the men here are brothers and cousins of your cacao cutters. Like all poor people, the cutters are perfectly willing to share. We've talked to them. And I've spoken to Larry. He says the reserve is large enough to accommodate a new partner without the current co-op members feeling any pain. And you'll be helping bring social democracy to the western world. Isn't that what you came here to do?"

"That's what Victor came here to do, and he already lived just down the road. I came a thousand miles to start a co-op, I think." *You've spoken to Larry?*

"And play baseball," Judy said dismissively.

That stung, and I knew I sounded weak, so I turned up the volume. "And although you, Victor and Larry seem to want to forget it, I'm still in the Peace Corps. How long do you think I'd last if Frank finds out that one of my principle investors is that enemy of the United States government, Che Guevara? No offense, don Che."

He just waved his cigar in silent dismissal of any affront.

Judy's voice rose to match my own. "He won't be your investor, Jack, I will. When your boss sees that Congressman Wickerman's daughter not only writes glowingly about your co-op in a national magazine, she invests in it, too, he'll pee in his pants with pleasure."

"He'll pee in his pants in surprise. Last time I looked you were more or less broke. Where are you going to find the money to invest?" I asked.

"Money is seldom a problem when you are the daughter of a congressman, Jack." Judy laughed like a school girl. "People are always ready to do you a favor. Besides, don't you enjoy the idea of using money from my father's red-baiting friends to capitalize this revolution? Larry and I are working things out. And I have some connections. I can help in ways other than money."

Che switched us back to Spanish. "This is a good plan, my motorcycle friend. The people of the northern frontier will thrive through the strength of your co-op, and you will be doing Victor and me a favor. I have long since given up the notion that you would join our cause, but if you can help us without hurting others, where is the harm? I have friends in other places, other countries, who want to help us, but how? They can't send money to my bank, because I have no bank. Perhaps they, too, can invest in your co-op. This gives you more money to sign up new members and buy cacao and banana futures. The payments to these investors can be made to safe deposit boxes controlled by Victor. You will become my bank, Jack, and I will help you grow and put money in the hands of the *campesinos* for medicine for their children and welfare for their sick and old. We all win. What do you think?"

* * *

A few weeks later I was called into the Peace Corps central office in San Jose along with Collette, John, Walt and the rest of the volunteers for our quarterly gamma globulin shots from Dr. Ernie and the semi-humiliating offering of stool samples to check for parasites. Collette actually came up positive, so while they took her to the hospital for more tests and medicine, I thought I'd pop in on Larry. I barely got me head inside the big door of the coffee storage house when I heard the noises upstairs.

It was unmistakable and familiar. "That's right. Give it to me. Give it to me," a woman's voice shouted.

CHAPTER 28

I sat on a painted wrought-iron bench in the park across from Larry's office staring up at a strangler fig sending its roots into a lethal embrace around a linden tree. I kept trying to think up Judy metaphors but came up empty, which made me even angrier. I waited long enough to be sure Larry was alone, then took the stairs two at a time and threw open his door.

"Jackson," Larry said brightly. "I didn't know you were in town. I'd have baked a cake or whatever Ticos bake. Whoa. Why are you looking at me like that? What the shit?"

I glanced at him and then at the battered leather couch that was clearly the scene of the crime. "Are you having an affair with Judy Wickerman? Could you possibly be so dumb?"

"Hold your horses, old buddy. The short answer is no. Victor is having an affair with Judy, and probably Che Guevara is having an affair with Judy. I'm just fucking her every now and then." He put both hands in the air in a gesture of surrender. "Cut me a little slack, will you? You know that woman better than I do. Man, I used to think Zelda led with her pussy, but Judy uses it like a weapon. It wasn't my idea, but what the hell, I'm a guy. That's what guys do."

"Yeah, well, let me remind you what else guys do. They shoot other guys who are fucking their girlfriend. And Victor is armed and dangerous."

Larry folded his hands on his desk like a school teacher. "Don't worry about Victor. We're solid. And he's a lot like Judy in a way. They both have lofty goals and don't mind making a few compromises to get them. If Victor can't be president of Costa Rica, he wouldn't mind being president of Nicaragua. Having a good-looking red-headed American wife sure wouldn't hurt. And if it means sharing his woman with people who can get him to the top, so be it. It's happened before. Ever hear of Juan Peron?"

"Are you saying he let Che sleep with Judy?"

"'Offered' is a better word. But nobody "lets" Judy do anything. You know that. Poor old Victor. I'm sure he'd love to see Judy as his first lady of Nicaragua, but Judy has the bar set a little higher than that. She wants to be to Che what Che was to Fidel—the power behind the throne. And by the way? Giving Judy and Che an investor position in the co-op may have been one of the smartest things you've ever done."

"I didn't have a hell of a lot of choice. But what do you mean?"

"I know you have mixed feelings about her, but Judy Wickerman is a winner. And now that she's got a horse in our race, she's going to do everything she can to make us winners, too. Already has, in fact. Thanks to her daddy, the man we all love to hate, she has tremendous connections and she's eager to use them. The more money she can make for us, the more she makes for her beloved revolution. She just got me in touch with a clothing distributor out of San Antonio that said they'd buy all the baby clothes Collette and her sewing clubs can turn out. They placed an initial order for a hundred pair of pajamas. That's all we got and more. Collette and that fat lady she works with are doing cartwheels all over Limon. And they should be. I'm putting together a bag of money for all the little ladies of the sewing machines. Want to take it to Collette for me?

* * *

Collette and I sat at a dock-side Limon restaurant eating ceviche, drinking white wine and trying to keep our hands off each other.

"Well, I guess I'm going to have to change my opinion of your old girlfriend, Jack," Collette said. "You and I are about to hand my gals more money than they normally see in a year. I still don't trust her as far as I can throw her, but I've got to admit, she came through. Is she going to make a lot of money, too?"

"Yes, five times as much, in fact. But John has shown me business isn't like baseball. There don't have to be winners and losers. Your sewing circles win, we get more money to sign up new members, Che wins and little kids in Texas are sleeping in cheap pj's. Would you like to make love?"

"Right here? Absolutely. But let's get those little wads of money into the hand of doña Esperanza and her gals first. The last time I saw that much dough was on one of my brother's drug dealers on the South Side. It makes me nervous."

We walked to the center of town where doña Esperanza and her seamstresses had prepared another feast for us. We weren't hungry, but nibbled on this and that out of respect. The women were clearly skittish, with that fatalism that poverty fosters. Was someone going to pull the rug out from under them again?

Doña Esperanza had asked Collette if the money could be distributed in small bills for a couple of reasons. First, the women could hand their husbands a stack of money and hide the rest. Second, they wanted small bills because the little stores they shopped at couldn't change big ones. Plus, walking around with a 100 *colone* bill (which is about $14) was just asking for it.

So when I handed the first woman 300 *colones* in fives, tens and twenties, she grabbed the pile tightly to her chest and burst into joyous tears. This made everybody else cry, of course, even Collette, who was gripping my arm so tightly she almost drew blood.

"It doesn't get any better than this, darling," she whispered.

"Oh yes it will. Let's get back to your apartment."

Collette and I made the long walk back to her apartment playing touching games and getting so sexually excited, I thought one or both of us might faint.

"I'm thinking of seven things that I'm going to do to you when I get you upstairs," Collette said in a husky voice.

"I can only think of one right now," I answered in what I thought of as my sexy voice. "I'm going to take off all your clothes and make long, lingering love to you."

She laughed that infectious roar that made people on the other side of the street turn and smile. "Wow. I never thought of that. Okay, eight things."

Collette's apartment was upstairs over a beauty parlor. I had only been there a couple of times before, and those were at night when I snuck in like a cat burglar. We'd been very circumspect, I thought, so what happened next unnerved me.

Collette's landlady, who also owned the beauty shop, came rushing out of the salon toward us, waving a telegram. "My God, miss Collette, at last, at last you have come. We did not know where you were. There is a telegram for you." She looked at her shoes shyly. "I am sorry. I read it. I think it is very important. Your doctor is coming. Your doctor is coming." She shot me a look of deep suspicion.

Collette took the telegram from the shaking hands of her landlady. "She's right, Jack, it's from Dr. Ernie. He wants me to meet him at the airport. He's coming in on the afternoon plane from San Jose."

The cab ride to the airport was quiet. Neither of us knew what to say. Finally Collette sighed and looked away from me. "So maybe I'm sicker than we thought. I thought I'd drink some paregoric and that would be that." She patted my hand. "I know I'm not pregnant, if that's what you're wondering."

Dr. Ernie led the other passengers down the off-ramp and took Collette's shoulders in his big hands. "Glad you got the message, Collette. Thanks for meeting me. Hi, Jack. I wasn't expecting to see you here."

"Just co-op stuff," I replied meekly. "Is everything okay?"

Dr. Ernie ushered us into the airport manager's office. He sat Collette down on the only chair, his hands still guiding her shoulders.

"Am I sick, Dr. Ernie? Do I have something bad?" she asked in a trembling voice.

"No, child, you're fine," Dr. Ernie said in his smoker's baritone. He looked at me and then back at Collette. "Perhaps you'd prefer if we were alone?"

"No, please let Jack stay," Collette said. "If I'm not sick, what is it?" Her eyes widened. "Is it my brother?"

"No, Collette, but it is very bad news. I'm afraid that your mother was killed yesterday in Chicago. I've asked the plane to wait for us, so we can get back to San Jose as quickly as possible. The Peace Corps will of course pay for your trip back for the funeral. We would have made all the arrangements, but we're having a little difficulty finding next of kin. You have a brother?"

She looked at me helplessly. "Oh shit, Jack." Then the tears stopped and the street-smart Collette came out of hiding. "Yes, Dr. Ernie, I've got two brothers. One's doing five to seven at Joliet. My other brother is thirteen, and probably sitting in that South Side apartment scared and hungry. He's all alone. And now I'm all he's got." She stood up and took my face in both of her hands. "It doesn't matter now, Jack. I can say I love you out loud. I'm not going back for the funeral. I'm going back, period. I'm going back to be the mommy. I love you, Jack. Let's go, Dr. Ernie."

CHAPTER 29

Just like that it was done. Got to hand it to the Peace Corps. Frank had Collette on the red eye to Houston that very night. Martha came into Limon to pack up Collette's stuff; Collette's erstwhile partner Jerry Festa said he'd rather eat ground glass than deal with the fat ladies and was transferred; and doña Esperanza said that was fine, she'd rather deal directly with the handsome American than the drunkard anyway. I thought at first she meant me, but she was really talking about Larry.

It was just as well. I was glad to hand the co-op reins to Larry and get out of Limon. The town was like a Collette museum to me. I saw her everywhere; heard her laugh, even smelled her soapy fragrance. I was crazy lonely and frankly didn't give a shit if the trains ran on time or not. I wrote her almost every day on those dumb little flimsy blue air mail deals that are both paper and envelope. I had her address, of course, and I even toyed with the idea of quitting and going to Chicago, but to be honest, she hadn't really asked me to join her. She was making the best of a bad deal, and didn't want to suck me down with her.

She left so fast, I didn't even have a picture of her. Absence of evidence.

I beat it back to San Isidro, intent on losing myself in the baseball league which had taken a back seat to the co-op. Mickey and Carlos had done okay keeping the league together, but they both had regular jobs. So I became baseball's Johnny Appleseed again, going from village to village—Upala, Rio Frio, Canalete, Bijagua, Los Chiles—repairing the back stops, liming the fields, building up pitcher's mounds, inventorying equipment. I flew back to San Jose and bought bats and balls, much to the delight of little Constantinopolis, who sort of attached himself to me on the days between LACSA flights.

Conti and I talked all the time. Either his accent or my Spanish had gotten a lot better since that first day I landed in San Isidro. He'd go with me on my rounds, me on the horse Victor had loaned me, him on one of the mules he borrowed from the civil guard—don Quixote and Sancho Panza tilting at boredom.

To tell the truth, Conti wasn't bored at all. Life was a constant source of wonder to him, and immensely funny. Everything and everybody made him laugh—bubbly, cascading chuckles and snorts that would sometimes break out in the middle of a word, making his already semi-invented Spanish all the harder to follow.

I just gave up and let Conti's persistent good humor wash over me. It felt good, and I really didn't have a choice. Of all the people on Conti's planet, I was the most amusing. When I mispronounced a word or got one wrong, he'd point his finger at me and collapse in mirth (when I once called soap "sopa," which means "soup" in Spanish, he laughed so hard he fell backward into the river. This, of course, made him laugh even harder).

Conti had invented an America for me to live in. "How many airplanes do you own?" he asked as we were wading our mounts through the knee-deep mud that would be almost a road in the dry season.

"None. I own one old car, that is all."

"Right," he giggled and winked conspiringly. "And you own no big houses and fuck no movie stars. You forget, don Shack, I have seen the movies. I have seen the movies." He laughed again in triumph.

We were putting away the horse and mule at the civil guard stable late one afternoon when Mickey came trotting across the bridge toward us. He was carrying the mail bag.

"Hey, Harjo, when will my duties for you ever end? Baseball coach, your personal LACSA agent, telegraph operator and now mailman." He brandished a small package wrapped in twine. "Here you are, my friend, special delivery all the way from Chicago."

"It is from one of your wives," Conti said, overcome by his brilliant comedic timing.

* * *

Costa Rica still didn't have street addresses or postal zones, so the package simply read "Jack Harjo, Peace Corps, C/O Mickey Munoz, San Isidro, Frontera Norte, Costa Rica." The handwriting was bold, the package was just the right size, even the Gordian knot was perfect. I just held it in my hand like a bird's nest for a long five seconds.

"Open it for me, will you, Mickey? I don't have a knife. And try not to cut the paper."

Inside was a five-by-seven photograph of Collette that must have been taken when she was at SMU. It was one of those yearbook glamour shots of pretty girls not quite smiling and not quite looking at the camera. This wasn't the Collette I knew, but it was better than nothing. There was another photo of her beaming that beautiful gap-toothed grin, wrapping her arm around a solemn young teenager, who the writing on the back revealed was her little brother Curtis. I've still got that one.

I also still have the letter that somehow retains traces of its eau de Collette. I pull it out and smell it all the time.

"Buenos días, mi amor," the letter begins. "Today is a very happy day for me, because not one, but three of your letters arrived this morning. They are such wonderful letters, Jack, and so filled with you and our life together in Costa Rica, a life that now seems so far away. You are such a gifted writer, it is clear you will be a great journalist someday. And Jack, to read that you love me moves me deeply. It is easy to say "I love you," especially in moments of passion, but to see it in writing feels like you going inside me for the first time, every time I read it. Thank you, my darling, I love you, too. I wish I had the power to express my love for you as you do for me.

"As you might imagine, I have been running a little low on happy days lately. Mother was gunned down while she was sitting on the front steps of our apartment house. The police said the neighbors saw a car drive slowly by; somebody rolled down a window and opened fire. They were probably aiming at someone else. The police have been nice, and say they are working on it; but they know, and I think they know I know, that this was just ghetto lightning, striking an innocent woman dead, and then rumbling away with the wind. They'll never catch the guys.

"It was lucky I got back as quickly as I did. The police either didn't know, or didn't check that Curtis had a big sister. Curtis is a little slow and doesn't talk much, so that probably didn't help. By the time I showed up, social services had already taken Curtis into custody and assigned him to a temporary foster care placement. You know what they call those foster care hell holes, Jack? 'Warm houses.' Jesus. It's like some people sat around and said, okay, what's the least appropriate name we can think of for these dumps? I got it—warm houses. Sorry, my darling. I spend a little bit of every day, too much, being angry at people I've never met and raging against the machine. See how important your letters are?

"The Peace Corps has been really nice. I've got about twelve hundred dollars back pay coming my way soon, which should get us through the winter. Dr. Ernie, bless his heart, loaned me $200 as I was getting on the plane, which I needed to show social services that I was financially capable of taking care of my brother. I had to go before a board of high school drop-outs to explain why I didn't have a job, and why I had been out of the country for a year. I was tempted to tell them that my boyfriend played baseball with Che Guevara, but for once I held my tongue. You would have been proud of me.

"I have been looking for jobs everywhere, sending out resumes to every corner of the globe. I'd very much like to get us out of Chicago, out of the South Side, but it may take a little while. I start next week part-time at the Tribune, working in circulation. It lets me be home before Curtis gets out of school, but it's just a job.

"I've told Curtis all about you, and he thinks meeting a cowboy Indian would be just fine. I think so, too. You've got a lot of very important work still ahead of you, darling, but when you come home, I want to be with you. Let me shout it from the roof tops: "I love Jack Harjo, and want to live with him for the rest of his life." Maybe when you get back, you'll get a job as a newspaperman in Oklahoma or Texas or Santa Fe or I Don't Give a Damn, Idaho. As long as we're together. As long as we're together.

"I love you more than all the sand in Puntarenas,

Collette

"P.S. Speaking of Texas, I sent my resume to that baby clothes wholesaler in San Antonio that was buying all our stuff. I thought maybe I could get a job in marketing or be a buyer. The letter came back "address unknown." So I called San Antonio information and got hold of Alamo Industries. Turns out there is an Alamo Industries, but the nice man explained that they sold oil field supplies and wouldn't know a baby dress from a Baby Ruth. Maybe I got the name wrong."

Then again . . .

CHAPTER 30

Like everybody else in the world, I remember precisely where I was and what I was doing.

It was late afternoon and I was sitting at one of the oilcloth-covered tables at the Buena Vista, watching the chocolate-colored Zappo River slip by. I was drinking a steaming mug of *café con leche* and enjoying a danish, taking advantage of the fact that the bread supply from San Jose had just come in that morning and the ants hadn't had time to plan their attack. It was quiet as only a jungle after the rain can be quiet.

Until it wasn't.

I heard the wailing, Banshee ululations (90) long before I saw him. Then Conti, blubbering and almost unintelligible, came running into the big open-air room. He had lost his baseball cap and he was pulling at his tee shirt like a madman, enlarging the hole in the front until there was little more than a collar and arms.

"They killed our president, don Shack. They killed him and now you must go home." He dropped to his knees in uncontrollable sobs.

I just stared at him for a second. I had never seen Conti cry, and the president of Costa Rica wasn't a very popular guy. Then I rose from the table as it dawned on me. In Conti's world, his president and my president were the same.

I started trotting down the cobblestone and mud main street to the air strip. As I passed Fonseca's barber shop, I heard funereal music on the radio and what sounded like moaning. I broke into a sprint.

Mickey was in the LACSA shack, his earphones on and taking notes as fast as he could scribble. Victor was standing behind him, fiddling with the short wave radio. He waved me in, then went back to intent listening.

We stood in the crackling and sputtering of the radio, looking back and forth in questioning stares. Finally, Mickey spoke into the microphone. "Understood. LACSA San Isidro out."

He wearily pulled off his headset and placed it in his lap. "So, it is true, Harjo. There is no easy way to tell you. This afternoon president John F. Kennedy was shot and killed in Dallas, Texas. And it may get much worse. Nobody seems to know anything. All LACSA flights to the United States have been cancelled. The same for the Canal Zone. I am very sorry, my friend."

I sat down hard on a bag of rice. "They shot Kennedy? Why would they do that? What do you mean, 'may get worse?' What could be worse?"

Victor twisted the big dial on the short wave, getting fragmented bursts of this, fleeting garbles of that. He kept staring into the radio as if that would make him hear more clearly.

"Damn, it's impossible to hold a signal in this jungle. But Jack, it looks bad; it looks very, very bad. I picked up Radio Havana a few minutes ago, and Castro has placed Cuba in a state of general mobilization. Cuban intelligence says that the assassination of Kennedy is just the beginning of a government coup in your country that will lead swiftly to an invasion of Cuba."

I flashed angry. "That's absurd, right? Somebody shoots our president, and Castro makes it about himself. That can't be. Why? Why?"

"It may be wrong; everybody seems to be in the dark." Victor looked at me in stern sadness. "But this is not some crazy new idea. Judy told us weeks ago that the word inside Washington was that Kennedy was preparing to lift the embargo against Cuba. She said the ultra-conservatives in Congress, including her father, the CIA, and the rich anti-Castro Cubans in Florida would never let it happen. 'Over his dead body' was exactly what she said, Jack, 'over his dead body.'"

I felt like I was going to faint. "I think I need to go back to Peace Corps headquarters. I, um, really don't know what to do. When is the next flight to San Jose, Mickey?"

"Maybe Tuesday, if the world is still in one piece."

* * *

Three days later I finally arrived in San Jose, and the entire country was in mourning. Kennedy had been the first United States president to visit Costa Rica, and he was wildly popular. There were Kennedy cigarettes, Kennedy candy bars, Kennedy pencils and pens, even Kennedy rum. The notorious night club/whorehouse Tio Sam's had a Tio Sam cocktail napkin autographed by Pierre Salinger framed and hanging in the entrance. There was no hard evidence that the president had ever been there, but rumors abounded.

It was no rumor that the people of Costa Rica were stunned and saddened by Kennedy's death. Costa Rican men and women are much more open with their emotions, and it deeply affected us, the button-down Americans, as we watched the Ticos, many in tears, display a grief we felt, but couldn't express.

San Jose was a grief magnet that week and it pulled dozens of Peace Corps volunteers into our main office, searching for answers, both professional and personal. Would there still be a Peace Corps, would it make any difference if I stay or go, what kind of America would I be returning to if I left?

Frank was absolutely no help; he wasn't even there. He was in Columbia with Tom Vaughn and some other Peace Corps bigwigs, leaving poor Dr. Ernie to minister to our doubts and fears. He tried his best, and for once didn't try to shrug it off with a joke.

"Look guys," he told a bunch of us who had congregated in the second-floor conference room, "The world will be here tomorrow; the United States will be here tomorrow; and just as importantly, at least in the short run, so will your villages. I've been to your villages. I've seen with my own eyes the important work you are doing. Don't drop the baton now. You won't be doing the memory of your president any good by turning your back on the one program he started from scratch. Cry. Hug each other. Have a beer. Then go back to your villages. Please."

The beer part sounded right to John, Walt and me, so we trudged off to Oldimar's. Somewhat to our surprise, the Bar Soda Palace was packed with Americans—ex-pats, tourists and Peace Corps volunteers like Martha, Jeannie and Jerry who had by-passed the Dr. Ernie lecture; even Larry Reznick showed up. There wasn't a banana split or guava milkshake anywhere in sight. Who eats ice cream at a funeral? Even the beers seemed more like movie props than drinks, people picking absent-mindedly at their labels as they listened to the radio.

We had Voice of America clear as a bell in San Jose, and when the three of us walked in, a military band was playing the Navy Hymn. It was tragic and beautiful and everybody was weeping. I don't cry, so I just leaned against a wall and sank slowly to the floor. I wanted so much to stay there.

Eventually, the music got replaced by yet another recap of the events, which we had all heard a dozen times. Oldimar snapped off the radio, and then, just like it said in our psychology 101 books, we moved through the stages of grief from sadness to anger.

"I know the rules," John announced to the assembled, "but does it have to be Lyndon Fucking Johnson? The Kennedys hated that cocksucker, no offense ladies, but it's true."

"Does it bother anybody else that Kennedy gets gunned down in Texas?" Larry asked. "Johnson owns that state. Owns it. And they say he killed a man once before when he was a congressman. Texas justice."

"Stop that, both of you," Jeannie said, sounding like an angry nun admonishing third-graders. "And you watch your mouth, Mister John McNaughton. I've had it with your schoolyard talk." Then, her resolve spent, she burst into tears, covered her face with her hands and slumped in her chair.

Larry walked by and tapped John and me on the shoulders. "Let's take ourselves over to my office for a rum punch and a little giggle grass," he said so only we could hear.

"Sounds righteous," John said, heading for the door. "As the man said as he was fucking the skunk, 'This is about as much fun as I can stand.'"

We got to Larry's coffee-fragrant office, where he cracked open a bottle of the ubiquitous *Flor de Caña* rum. I grabbed one of the chairs. There was no way I was going to sit on that carnal sofa, thank you very much. Larry rolled a joint, took a hit, and started talking to the ceiling. "So what are you guys going to do? Are you going to quit the Peace Corps? I need to know, because with you or without you, I want to keep on running the co-op. This is the first time in my life where I think I can do good and do well at the same time."

I thought of Collette. "I'm not a quitter, and on top of that, I don't know exactly where I'd wind up if I did leave. Besides, if Victor and Judy are right, the government could be topsy-turvy in a little while and, hell

I don't know, maybe Arthur Wickerman will be president of the United States." I took a healthy swig. "In which case, I'll probably be playing jungle baseball for the rest of my life."

"I'm not going anywhere," John said, suddenly serious. "Governments get overthrown in banana republics, but not the United States. Never has happened and never will. Victor's probably talking about our government being overthrown because he's dead set on overthrowing one himself. He's trying to justify his own actions by making it look like it's all the rage, like the Beatles.

"And speaking of bananas, I've taken a real shine to my banana growers. They work like dogs, never complain and die before they're fifty. They need the money we're giving them bad, and I feel like I'm finally doing something besides pontificating. I only wish we had some more money to invest. I've got growers standing in line to join, but I've seen the books and we're doing okay, but not great." He flashed a huge grin as he blew a smoke ring. "Yes, goddam it, I'm aware that I pontificate."

"Access to capital is exactly why I wanted to talk with you fellows," Larry said. "I had actually planned to discuss this with you before all hell broke loose. I've already spoken to Victor and Judy about it. They think it's a great idea. In fact it was sort of Judy's idea in the first place. Now, Jackson, don't shut your mind on this. It's the message, not the messenger."

He was right. I was already thinking up reasons not to like whatever was coming. Larry knew me well.

John set his little glass of rum down and gave Larry his full business-school attention. "What are you talking about, Larry? Why the build-up?"

Larry leaned forward. "You are absolutely right, John. We are doing okay, but we could be doing so much more. Did you know that your buddy Walt is just raring to go with a co-op of those cart makers of his? We don't even have enough money to sign up the people in our three towns, much less take on additional sites. We need investors, gentlemen; new investors with new infusions of capital. You know the old business adage, John, 'grow or die.' I choose to grow, and I know you do, too." He took a tiny sip of his rum, more for theatrics than thirst, I thought. I knew Larry well, too.

"I have access to new investors, investors with large amounts of money. Now before you say anything, Jack, let me assure you that what I'm about to suggest is perfectly legal here in Costa Rica. It might be a gray area if we were in the states, but we're not. And if we can help hundreds, maybe thousands of people, I think we should consider this."

"When people say something is perfectly legal, it usually means it's not," John grumbled. "What is the 'this' you're talking about?"

"Some of my former business associates in Panama, you know who I'm talking about, are in need of investing in businesses that pay dividends. They are willing to invest heavily in our co-op and let us keep twenty-five percent of the money that flows through. We can sign up new members, build up our reserves, pay Victor, Che and Judy and our other investors handsomely and absolutely nobody gets hurt. What do you think?"

"I think that for all your predictions to the contrary, marijuana is still against the law in the United States," I answered. "If the Peace Corps caught me dealing drugs, I'd be out on my butt so fast I wouldn't know what hit me. And there would probably be some guy in Houston waiting for me with a badge and handcuffs. I think I'll sit this one out."

Larry chuckled. "That's the beauty of this plan, boy from Oklahoma. The marijuana has already been sold, probably to some folks in New York who are eating donuts and dancing to the weather report. It's harmless fun, but will have absolutely nothing to do with us in any case. We take the money, put it to its best possible use, and return a portion to our investors, including these guys. Nobody gets hurt and everybody wins."

John rubbed his chin. "I've read about this. It's called money laundering, I think. The drug dealers have tons of money, but they can't just bring sacks of it to their local banks without arousing suspicion. Then they get caught for tax evasion. That's what they finally nailed Capone for, as I remember. Are you sure this isn't against the law in Costa Rica?"

"You forget that I have majors in business law and Latin American studies, among others," Larry said. "I studied this thoroughly. This is so new there's not even a word for it in Spanish, much less a statute."

John turned to face me. "I don't think we should reject this out of hand, Jack. This has real merit, and could move the co-op from marginal to flush. We might be dealing with bad men, but as the Jesuits say, 'We will be cleansing the money by our acceptance of it.'"

"I never know when you're just making those quotes up. I don't know; let me think about it."

CHAPTER 31

There go my alarm chickens again. One of these days I'm going to have to ask them how they know when it's ten minutes before sunup. Maybe they're smarter than I think.

When I was a kid I used to talk to our chickens. I'd stand just outside the chicken-wire fence and explain how I had been misunderstood, mistreated, malnourished and maligned. I reminded them that other kids got to stay up until ten, did not have to clean their plates before they could have any dessert, could wear their Levis any darn way they pleased and why home work was stupid, especially on Fridays.

Mostly these talks were in the form of finger-pointing lectures and got the indifference they deserved. There was one brood hen, however, that seemed to understand, even sympathize. My mother was the smartest and most understanding woman I knew, but she spent three days a week at the newspaper. So I made that brood hen Mother's stand-in. Sometimes I'd ask her advice. She'd listen carefully, cock her head in thought, and then look at me wisely. And often, darned if the answer didn't just come bubbling to the surface.

When I returned to San Isidro, I spent quite a bit of time among my chickens looking for a wise and sympathetic hen to talk to. I had no one else. Collette was gone, and in any case I didn't feel good about putting Larry's plan into a letter. John had moved into Larry's camp, and just as Larry had said, when I returned to Che's compound for one of our baseball games, Victor, Judy and Che were not only enthusiastic, they talked about it like it was a done deal.

That left Conti. "Do you think there is such a thing as a greater good?" I asked absent-mindedly one morning as we rode a jungle trail. Maybe it was my Spanish, but Conti wasn't having any part of it.

"Good is good, don Shack, but how can there be a good that is better than good? Maybe there are little goods like fried platanos, and big goods like the baby Jesus. Is that what you mean?"

"More or less," I said and thought about the dead baby in my arms the year before. Why did Conti have to mention baby Jesus? I'm not particularly religious, but that's who I thought of when I held the little thing in my hands. It was a conundrum (10). Would I launder marijuana money to prevent another dead baby? Would laundering marijuana money prevent another dead baby, or was that just an excuse? I hunched forward in my home-made saddle and for the first time in ages longed for my wise, understanding and self-destructive mother. Or at least an attentive hen.

Then like so many others times in my life it seems, fate spared me the trouble of making up my mind. Instead it smashed into me head-first like a stop sign on D Street.

One morning a couple of weeks before Christmas, Conti and I trotted into Canalete to be met by a bare field. My starched and ironed friend Carlos, who usually had his team standing at parade rest waiting for me, was missing. So was everybody else.

"What's going on?" I asked. "Where is everybody?"

Conti pointed to the municipal building where the large sacks of rice, beans and cacao were stored, waiting for the dry season and the trucks. It was the largest building in the village and served double-duty as a movie theater on Saturday nights. "Over there."

I walked into the large and crowded hall, my Wellington boots ringing on the wooden floor of the suddenly-hushed room. You could tell that conversation had just been sucked out of the place, like when you walk back to your table and realize the other guests were talking about you. Carlos rushed up to me with the eyes of a basset hound and grabbed my hand in a two-handed shake.

"I am so sorry, don Juan, so very sorry."

I had grown a little tired of this. "Thank you, Carlos, my friend, but there is no need. President Kennedy has been dead a month. It is time to put old sadness behind us."

"I wish it were that easy," Carlos said wearily. "Please come with me." He led me to a small table where a few cacao pods were scattered, picked one up and using a machete like I would a pocket knife, sliced it open.

Cacao is a strange-looking plant, and like the oyster, makes you wonder how hungry the first guy must have been when he took his first bite. Cacao beans come in eight-to-ten-inch pods that look like squash, but grow on trees. After the pods are cut from the trees, the pod is cut open. Inside, the buckeye-size cacao beans, maybe twelve to the pod, lay in a gooey white cream. They are removed and placed on huge drying racks that stink to high heaven, but get the job done. The purple dried bean is unbelievably bitter until it is ground to a powder and cut with sugar. Then it becomes cocoa.

But not these pods. Cacao pods are kind of pretty as a rule, yellow-orange with daubs of green and touches of red. The pods arrayed in front of Carlos looked like week-old bananas, with a dark bruise going up one side. When Carlos laid his pod open, the drying-rack stink had sunk inside the pod with a dead-dog odor that once smelled, can never be forgotten. The beans were withered and the creamy cover had changed to a yellow soup with streaks of black.

Conti gasped and backed away, crossing himself. "Witch's broom," he whispered.

"What in the hell is that?" I asked, as a dozen men sitting around the room murmured and sadly nodded in agreement with Conti's diagnosis.

"It is as he says, my friend, the black pod disease, what we call witch's broom." Carlos could see I was having trouble keeping up with words I had never heard before describing something I had never seen before, so he spoke more slowly.

"It is a fungus. You understand fungus? It is a fungus that gets in the soil and then in the trees. The wind blows it here and there and it kills everything it touches. It is in Canalete today, but could be in San Isidro in only days. It is a killer spore. You understand the word spore? It is like a tiny mushroom that you cannot see or taste that dances on the wind. It is a dance of death." Carlos put the stinking pod down on the table. "It even smells like death."

"I never heard of such a thing. Can it be stopped? Can anything be done?"

"Yes, I remember that we fought it and won in 1947," Carlos said. "But it takes a terrible toll. We will lose this year's crop, we will lose many trees, and we must apply copper sulfate, which is very expensive." He snapped his fingers in that curious Latin-American way that looks like your fingers have turned into the end of a whip.

"I'm very sorry, Carlos, sorry for all of you." I extended my arm in a sweeping motion to include the room.

Carlos looked at me like I might be slightly retarded. "You are very much the gentleman, which we all knew, but you must also have concern for yourself, don Juan. You see those sacks? Half of them belong to the co-op, to OTABCO. That is a good thing. But look out the window. See the trees? See the pods? OTABCO owns half of them, too, and they must be cut down and burned. The co-op paid most of us for our crops month by month, but now the harvest time is here and the pods must be destroyed. We have no cacao and little money. We must apply the sulfate and replant. Can OTABCO help us again? It will be life blood for us."

I put my arm around Conti, who seemed to be growing smaller by the minute. "Let me see what I can do. We will think of something."

* * *

I sat in Larry's office and explained our disaster. "So we will be able to get maybe a quarter of our expected cacao crop to market," I said. "And that's not the worst part. We've got to find some money to help our members replant and get through the growing months or there will be no cacao next year either. We'll go belly up and so will our cutters. You probably know what I'm about to ask: can we do some business with your Panamanian grass guys?"

Larry clasped his hands and leaned forward on his elbows until he was half-way across his desk. "No worries, as our old friend Nigel used to say. I saw this coming months ago. Well, maybe not this specifically, but something." He leaned back in his chair. "Now don't over-react, Jack, but I've actually been doing this for months. I just offered it as a plan last month because I wanted it to seem like your idea. And now it is. We've got plenty of money to take care of this, just like we had the money to buy Collette's ugly little baby clothes."

"So that's why Alamo Industries told Collette they didn't know what she was talking about."

Larry laughed. "There actually is an Alamo Industries? Judy and I just made that up. We figured San Antonio, you know, and all that shit; it sounded natural."

"I'm glad Collette didn't know. What about John? He said he looked at the books and we were only okay. Is he in on it?"

Larry laughed again, but the humor had drained out of this one. "My dear old friend, how did you keep from drowning in the rain along with all the other turkeys? John saw one set of books, what I call my Peace Corps books. There may be another set."

CHAPTER 32

In the early morning hours of January 14, 1964, Victor Victorin was shot and killed at the army garrison of Matagalpa, Nicaragua. His bullet-ridden body, along with two of his commanders, Miguel Arias and Roberto Sarria, was tied to a plank and exhibited like an Old West desperado on the garrison steps.

It was a quick, bloody and fruitless revolution in a country famous for bloody and fruitless revolutions. Most people in the capitol of Managua weren't even aware of it until they saw the grisly photos in *La Nation* the next day. None of the news articles carried any mention of Che Guevara.

Victor and his men had taken their boats up the Grande de Matagalpa River, confident that the First Regular Warfare Battalion, which was strongly rumored to be against Somoza, would join forces with Victor's commandos and secure the garrison. In fact, the Second Company did just that, and together they captured the main buildings and one of the barracks. But other company commanders hesitated, watching which direction the winds of war would blow, and the revolution stalled. In less than twelve hours, troops loyal to Somoza, in armored vehicles still bearing the markings of the US Army, stormed the garrison and cut the insurgents to ribbons. Only a few of Victor's men, mostly sentries left behind with the boats, made it back to Che's compound.

I got most of my information from the cacao cutters in San Isidro, who were feverishly topping and trimming trees and treating the soil with copper sulfate. So far it seemed to be working.

I couldn't help noticing that the number of cutters was swelling, which was welcome, but surprising. I recognized a few of the new faces as some of the baseball players on Che's team; men who had enough of fighting and were returning to their cousins, uncles and friends, hoping to disappear in the jungle.

Mickey and I pitched in cutting and pruning the cacao trees, listening as the men talked about the aborted garrison take-over, which was now common knowledge all over the villages that fronted the Nicaraguan border.

"It is completely over," the man I recognized as Juanito said. He was the same man I saw being treated by Guevara months earlier. "How could it have happened so fast? It is a ghost camp now. Old Casimiro trots around the buildings as if nothing has happened, but everybody else is on the wind. El Che and some of the men he brought with him have gone. It is said that they are on their way to Bolivia, where the fire of revolution is still burning, but I don't know. I do know that he was angry with us, blaming us for not caring as much about the people as he did."

"What about the woman," I asked too casually. Mickey shot me a knowing glance.

"The Pink Whore? Yes, she is still with El Che, to his everlasting sorrow, I believe."

I noticed that Judy had come down a few pegs, from lady to whore. "Why do you believe she will bring Che sorrow?" I just couldn't leave this alone.

Juanito flashed in anger. "That whore is the reason our dear comrade don Victor is dead. She filled him with lies and false promises. She is the devil."

A man relaxing near Juanito rose on one elbow. "She is worse than the devil. He only had an apple. The whore's fruits were more tempting to a man and more available." The group broke up in laughter. I felt my face color in a shame I'm sure Judy never felt.

"She was the great liar," an older man said. "I heard her tell El Che and Victor that the time to strike was now. The United States is about to have its own revolution, she said, and won't lift a finger to help The Frog. She took picture after picture of Victor, Che and their men with that big camera of hers. I could see that Victor believed her, and I think Che wanted to. El Che was tired of sitting in the jungle waiting, I think."

"She had a camera?" I asked. "I thought Che wouldn't let her bring a camera to the camp."

"That was before the book," Juanito spat. "That fucking book. She told El Che that she was writing a book that would convince all the gringos at last that he was the greatest revolutionary of all time, Marti and Bolivar and Washington in one package. All day she would follow him with her notebook, saying 'that is brilliant' and 'they will love this' and other things. I think El Che was flattered. What man would not be? El Che is very, very smart, but he has a soft spot for the ladies."

"Especially redheaded Americans, I am thinking," the older man said. "Maybe this will turn out well, but when you dance with the devil . . ."

* * *

A week later I was back in San Jose, looking for more money for the cacao cutters. Because everything was strictly on a cash basis these days, the only way I could get the money was to go to Larry's office and leave with a gym bag of dough.

When I got to the office, Larry's back was to me as he counted a small stack of *colones*. "That's the right idea, but I'm going to need more than that," I said jauntily.

Larry flinched, then turned to face me. His face was puffy and the color of black pod disease. "Yes you will, Jackson," he said thickly. "You just don't know it yet."

"Oh my god, Larry. What in the hell happened to you?"

"Well, you learn in business law that sometimes the fuckor becomes the fuckee." He tried to smile, then winced. "Our old buddy Judy and two of her bandoleros came in yesterday afternoon and stole every penny—'liberated it,' as she put it. One of the little shits actually stuck a gun in my face. That totally pissed me off and I cold-cocked him with a coffee mug. The next thing I remember it was the middle of the night and I was lying on the floor."

"I think you're lucky to be alive. I think Judy and Che are making a run for Bolivia. What were you thinking, partner? It's only money."

Larry sat heavily on his sofa of love. "That's what they say in the movies. But sometimes real life gets in the way. Judy knew exactly when the Panamanians would make their drop, and timed it perfectly. I was hip-deep in dollars when they showed up. We are wiped out, Harjo. And these bad guys are going to want their money. They will ask me where their $20,000 went, I'll tell them that Che Guevara stole it, and they will shoot me in the face. I'm getting out of here, and I don't mean tomorrow. I'm leaving on the ten o'clock to Bogota, and then we'll see. And Jack, you need to get out, too. There is still a couple of thousand bucks in the bank that only you can sign for. Take it, go back to you village and pack up your things, then get the hell out of Dodge. We're toast."

"What do you mean, toast? We can get their money back, Larry. It'll take longer, but I'm sure we can do it."

Larry pushed a manila envelope across the desk at me. "Toasted on both sides. Judy left this for you. It's a feature article she has written for *Newsweek*. There's also a letter. Yes, I read every damn word of them both. She says the entire disaster of a revolution was funded by marijuana money and she names you as the architect. Seems she just can't leave a place without breaking all the windows."

"Toast," I mumbled and, grabbing the envelope, staggered across the street to find a park bench and start reading.

CHAPTER 33

I fumbled with the fat envelope and read Judy's letter first. It was in her no-nonsense block printing that would reveal little to a handwriting expert, which was probably her plan.

"Dear Jack," she wrote, "By the time you read this I will be in New York with my editors putting the finishing touches on my feature-length article for *Newsweek.* My editors say this is killer stuff and have given me an advance to fly to South America to finish my book. I will also be able to help that magnificent man Che Guevara finish the revolution that never got off the ground in Nicaragua. I feel terribly sorry for Victor, of course, but for all of his sweet zeal, revolutions cannot be won in penny loafers.

"My editors are delighted and simply can't believe that I spent so much time with Che, chronicling a revolution from inception to bloody end." It dawned on me as I read that if Victor hadn't been riddled with bullets in Matagalpa, Judy wouldn't have had her bloody end, or any end for that matter. Maybe that was just the cynical journalist worming his way out of the swampy regions of my brain, but could that have been why she urged Victor to strike? Because she was on deadline?

"I feel very sorry that one of my men hurt Larry, but I am not the least bit sorry that we extracted his dirty money for the greater good of freeing the people. You must admit that there is poetic justice in using the capitalists' own love of drugs, their lust for power, drugs and money, to fund the very revolution that will send the capitalist pigs squealing into their mansions, begging for mercy." I only hoped that her article was better-written than that last sentence. That was one angry pink lady.

"Because you and I go back a long way, I feel like I owe you a head's up," she continued. "My editors kept pressing me for details of the machinery that goes into running a revolution, especially how we got our money. So I told them truthfully that the lion's share of the funding came from a scheme to launder marijuana money through your co-op. The editors were incredulous. 'You mean the same guy that was on our cover last year as the ideal Peace Corps volunteer was actually using the Peace Corps to launder marijuana money?' So I'm afraid the story isn't just about Che anymore. My editors think you may have broken several laws, both in Costa Rica and the United States, so you may want to take precautions."

The letter went on for a couple of more pages, but it was mostly righteous self-justification and more power-to-the-people bullshit. And to be honest, I had lost all my powers of concentration. I pulled the article out of the envelope, read it and then went back to Larry's now-abandoned office and wrote a long letter to Collette. Down deep I felt she would forgive me. I wasn't so sure about the rest of the world.

I went to the post office, then to the bank where I withdrew $1,800 in dollars. I wanted to fly to Chicago then and there, but it was Saturday and my passport was locked up in the Peace Corps office. So I flew that rattle-trap DC-3 back to San Isidro to pick up some papers, photos of my folks and Collette, say goodbye to Conti and then do exactly what Larry told me to do—blow the country. I had no idea it would be my last flight.

* * *

Judy Wickerman's 10,000 word article, "My Year With Che," caused a sensation. Judy had just spent more time with Che Guevara than any other American, ever. There were a dozen photographs of her and Che clowning with cigars, Victor and other guerrillas festooned with ammo belts and rifles, and an adoring portrait of a steely-eyed Che that was meant to be sexy and scary. In a lengthy side-bar, there was the same damn picture of me and Mickey that had graced the cover of *Newsweek* the year before, along with the subhead "Banking, Baseball and Marijuana?"

Advance galley proofs of the article were sent to the CIA, the House Foreign Relations Committee and, of course, the Peace Corps. Sargent Shriver, I understand, went apeshit, which was mild compared to the reaction of Oklahoma Congressman Arthur Wickerman, who was a ranking member of the foreign relations committee. Wickerman immediately called for congressional hearings on the Peace Corps. He hated the Peace Corps almost as much as he hated me, and to bring us both down with one swat was sweet. He went on record accusing me of seducing his daughter to join the Peace Corps, introducing her to Guevara, and then supplying her with drugs and money under the very noses of Peace Corps officials. Frank Le Pommes was summoned to Washington where he threw me to the wolves, of course. He said I had wandered off the reservation (those weren't really the words he used; he was dumb, but a gentleman) and was not only acting alone, but keeping two sets of books—one for the Peace Corps and one for the Panamanian drug lords. Frank retired a few weeks later.

John McNaughton was called before the committee and did his best to protect me. He expressed disbelief about the money laundering and showed contracts between the co-op and the American Fruit Company that exonerated him, and in fact had my signature on them. Collette gave tearful testimony that I was a man of integrity who had changed the lives of dozens of women for the better. She was afforded so little credibility she was in and out of the hearing in less than fifteen minutes. Then Wickerman called my name and told the assembled reporters that the Peace Corps needed to produce me within 72 hours or I would be in contempt of Congress. They didn't and I was.

I heard all this long after the fact, of course.

When the plane took off from San Isidro Saturday afternoon, there was nothing for me to do except attend to my personal affairs until LACSA returned on Tuesday. I had dinner with Mickey at the Buena Vista and showed him the article.

He read it carefully and then folded it back in its envelope. "Looks like you could be in trouble, my friend. Maybe big trouble. Did you actually have a money laundering deal going on?"

"Yes, Mickey, I did. Evidently, I did long before I knew I did, but that's beside the point. I did it for all the right reasons, but that's beside the point, too, isn't it? Larry promised me that it's not against the law in Costa Rica, but I knew it was wrong. I've got a hunch this is going to get me kicked out of the Peace Corps, and I feel rotten about that."

"Let's try and stay focused on what's important, shall we?" Mickey said sternly. "Does this mean I have to give back my OTABCO baseball jersey?"

We both collapsed in laughter.

* * *

On Monday morning Mickey came trotting over to the medical unit where Conti and I were feeding my chickens. The chickens had grown sleek and fat, and Conti took pride in what he now considered at least partly his brood.

Mickey was looking all business. "You are a lucky guy, Harjo. Remember when you first came here and told me that you were expected to help build an all-weather road? Well today you can thank heaven that the only way in and out of here is by plane, and LACSA doesn't come until tomorrow. That gives you some time."

That unnerved me a little. "Time to what?"

He held up the folded and sealed papers I recognized as telegrams. "Look, I've got two telegrams here. One is for you, and the other is about you, and they both are bad."

"Is it from the Peace Corps?" I asked in resignation.

"Yes, it is from that nice Dr. Ernie guy telling you to return to Peace Corps headquarters in San Jose immediately. It doesn't say anything else, which makes it ominous, like the dog that doesn't bark." He waved one of the papers. "But the other one says plenty, and you are in very bad trouble. This one is from the Civil Guard headquarters telling Corporal Mendoza to take you into custody and fly with you tomorrow to the Civil Guard facility in Alajuela."

I was shocked. "Why? Larry told me that money laundering was not a crime in Costa Rica. That rat."

"I do not know about that, but selling drugs is. Somebody, maybe your friend Judy, tipped the police that there were drugs in your office in San Jose."

"That's not my office. That's Larry's office."

"They will probably sort that out later. But they found marijuana in it. You have been charged with selling drugs, which can put you in a Costa Rican jail for seven years. The minute you step off that plane tomorrow, you are going straight to prison."

Conti started to cry, which didn't help anything. "But I didn't; I can't; I mean, well, what can I do?" I muttered and put my arm around Conti so I wouldn't cry myself. I was really scared, for the first time in my life. I had the crazy and fleeting thought that soon Collette would have both her brother and her boyfriend in prison.

Mickey gave me a smile of reassurance. "I have to deliver this telegram to Corporal Mendoza, but not right away. I'll give it to him late this afternoon, just before his supper. He is fat and lazy and besides he has no place to put you. He will not come looking for you until tomorrow. That gives you some time. Why don't you disappear for a few days until I can find out what this is all about."

"But where would I go? I am wanted by the federal police."

Conti straightened up and danced in front of us, his goofy smile broader than ever. "I know where, don Shack, I know where. They only want you in Costa Rica. You can go to Nicaragua and live in old man Casimiro's camp. I think it is empty again. Don't worry. Casimiro is my uncle."

CHAPTER 34

Asunción, Paraguay
September 15,1964

My dearest Collette,

Well, I made it. New name (were you surprised to see a letter from Jack Hogan?), new passport (I'm a Canadian now, eh?), and a new future in a new city. Life is looking up at last.

I'm sorry to not have written for the past few weeks, but getting here was a roller coaster. I was always on the move and staying as low and out of sight as I could. But no complaints.

As I told you in my last letter, Mickey finally made contact with an old merchant marine buddy in Limon who was the captain of a Liberian freighter. The man told Mickey that if I could make it to Bluefields, he would pick me up on his next trip and drop me off in Cartagena. I got the passport in Bluefields (I think it looks lousy, but it got the job done), which set me back plenty. The captain was true to his word, but he set me back plenty, too, and to tell the truth, I discovered I'm not the world's greatest sailor. From Cartagena I took a five-day bus ride through

Venezuela and Brazil that wound through every Amazon village and a few of the most treacherous mountain passes I've ever seen. Apparently chickens ride free in South America, because my buses were always full of them.

I arrived in Asuncion with less than two hundred dollars to my name, which by the looks of it, still makes me middle class. Actually, it's a very pretty city of about 300,000 people, right across the Paraguay River from Argentina. It is springtime now, with flowering trees everywhere. I think you will like it, and it's bound to be prettier than I Don't Give a Damn, Idaho (I love you, girl).

So here's the latest news from police blotters around the world: the government of Costa Rica has dropped its marijuana smuggling case against me. According to Oldimar, who wrote me occasionally, even though my name was on the lease for the office, they couldn't tie the brick of grass to me. He said it might also have had something to do with the fact that the grass disappeared from the Civil Guard evidence room only a few days after it got there. Some die-hard Costa Rican prosecutor wanted to get me for stealing from the co-op, but John McNaughton, who took over the co-op after I left, said the money was actually mine to begin with and refused to press charges.

The contempt of Congress charge went away, too, when Wickerman's Peace Corps hearings ended. "Harjo" is still a dirty word around Peace Corps headquarters, but Jack Hogan is tabula rasa.

The only legal mess I'm still in came out of left field. Larry told the truth for once that money laundering wasn't a crime yet in Costa Rica. It is in the United States, however, and because I was a United States citizen in Costa Rica as a federal employee, I have been charged with money laundering in the District of Columbia. It's a tough one, and I could get up to five years in federal prison if I'm found guilty. I'm not sure I'm ready to go to the slammer for a victimless crime where the only people who got burned were Panamanian drug dealers. We can talk about it.

I wrote my dad (Jack Hogan doesn't say daddy) and asked him what he thought of me changing my name. He said it was fine, that Indians did it all the time. You get one name when you are born, then when you are a man, you get your warrior name, which is either picked for you by a chief or you pick it yourself. He said paying respect to Old Bob that way was a good idea, although he was kind of hoping I'd call myself Eagle Feather after my motor scooter.

Speaking of Dad, I asked him to transfer $5,000 from my trust fund to the co-op, which is still going strong. Although all the other volunteers from our group finished their two years in July (!), John agreed to stay on for a few more months to keep the co-op going and groom a successor. John signed another contract with American Fruit, Carlos got some cacao to market, and as far as I know doña Esperanza is still turning out baby clothes. You probably know more about that than I do. I also asked Dad to send a thousand dollars to Mickey to give to Conti. Mickey agreed to pay Conti 100 colones a month to take care of my chickens. That should put some walk-around money in Conti's pocket for a few years.

I'm going to ask Dad to send me the rest of my trust fund so I can get started in business. The statute of limitations on money laundering is seven years, and I want to do something fun and productive while I'm waiting. There is an English-language newspaper down here, The Asuncion Herald, that is for sale. It isn't much of a paper right now, only 2,000 circulation, but heck, The Ardmorite back in my home town wasn't much bigger than that when I was a kid. Plus I will have a Chicago Tribune-trained circulation manager if things fall my way.

Mickey got word to me that he sent you a whole box of examination blue books that I've been using to write my memoirs, I'd guess you'd call them. I hope you get them. I'm thinking about using them as the basis for a book, a book that probably nobody except the two of us will believe. I've already got a title—"Che Guevara's Marijuana and Baseball Savings and Loan." What do you think? Too long? We've got time to work on it.

I hope you and Curtis will join me. I know it's a long way from the South Side of Chicago, but isn't that part of its charm? There's an American school for all the embassy and expat kids so Curtis could hit the ground running. Please come to Paraguay. I miss you. I need you. I love you.

Jack

OLD BOB'S LIST OF WORDS

1. Abstemious—moderate; not self-indulgent, like my first wife.
2. Avuncular—kind and friendly; like an uncle, or me.
3. Autarchy—despotism.
4. Banal—feeble, commonplace. See Wickerman, A.
5. *Bête noire*—a person or thing one particularly dislikes or fears. See Wickerman, above.
6. Bodkin—a blunt, thick needle, or a pick editors use to remove bad type.
7. Caduceus—twin-snaked wand of Hermes, symbol of medicine.
8. Charisma—an attractive aura; great charm.
9. Conjugal—marriage; something you and Glenda better stay away from.
10. Conundrum—a riddle, or puzzling situation.
11. Coup—a successful stroke or play. You'd be surprised how many people think this has something to do with Chevrolets.
12. Decimate—kill or remove a large portion. It literally means to kill ten percent of the enemy, but it got a little fuzzy with use.
13. Desiccate - remove the moisture from.
14. Desultory- half-hearted, disconnected.
15. Diaphanous—light and delicate.
16. Dichotomy—a sharp contrast between opposites. It doesn't mean dilemma.
17. Ellipsis—an omission from a sentence of words needed to complete a thought. It is indicated by three dots. Everybody has seen the three

dots; nobody knows what they are called.

18. Emasculate—deprive of force; castrate. What my second wife tried to do to me.
19. Ennui—boredom.
20. Fatuous—silly, idiotic, Wickerman-like.
21. Finial—that thingamabob on the top of lampshades and pedestals. Remember, Jack, everything has a name.
22. Fulcrum—the middle point where teeter-totters neither teeter nor totter.
23. Gaffe—a blunder; not the barbed hook you use to land big fish (that's a gaff).
24. Genuflect—bend the knee in worship.
25. Glottis—windpipe. Don't confuse it with the epiglottis, which is that little doohickey at the root of your tongue (not that you would, of course).
26. Gyre—a whirling or vortex. Not just a made-up word in "Jabberwocky."
27. Halcyon—calm, peaceful.
28. Hegemony—leadership or dominance. Use this word with nations, not people.
29. Helix—a spiral curve, like a corkscrew or a watch spring.
30. Hibernian—an Irishman. Now you know where the Hibernia Bank started.
31. Homage—great respect or reverence. Almost always used as "pay homage."
32. Hubris—arrogance or excessive pride that will lead to one's downfall. Literally it means "defiance of the gods," which will fuck you up.
33. Ignominy—dishonor, infamy. Not to be confused with ignoramus or Republican, which mean the same thing.
34. Insouciant—carefree, unconcerned; most often used negatively, like the grasshopper, not the ant.
35. Jejune—shallow, intellectually unsatisfying. See Wickerman, A.
36. Jeroboam—a wine bottle four times ordinary size. Thank god Four Roses doesn't come in this size.
37. Juxtapose—place things side by side for comparison.
38. Karabiner—a coupling link used by mountain climbers. Has nothing to do with guns.
39. Kiln—a furnace or oven primarily used for firing pottery. Pronounced "kill."

40. Kismet—destiny, fate.
41. Lachrymose—tearful, weepy.
42. Lacuna—a gap, blank or missing portion. Most often applied to ancient books or manuscripts.
43. Lambent—softly radiant, like a flame playing on a surface, or fireflies at night. I love this word.
44. *Lese-majesty*—treason, or an insult to the ruler.
45. Louche—disreputable, shifty; see Wickerman, A.
46. Lumbar—your lower back area. Has nothing to do with wood.
47. Masticate—chew. You were thinking Playboys in the bathroom, right?
48. Mendacious—lying, untruthful.
49. Missal—book of prayer, especially those used in Catholic Mass.
50. Moribund—lacking vitality, at the point of death.
51. Mufti—plain clothes worn by somebody usually in uniform, like a general playing golf.
52. Nadir—the lowest point. Usually used to mean deep despair.
53. Nimbus—halo, heavenly aura.
54. Noisome—harmful, noxious, evil-smelling, offensive. Has nothing to do with sound.
55. Obsequious—servile, like Uriah Heep.
56. Octavo—a book size obtained by folding a standard sheet three times to get eight pages. Octa- anything is going to mean eight.
57. Opossum—you know what it is; I know what it is; everybody knows what it is. How come nobody ever spells or pronounces it right?
58. Ostracize—exclude, banish; refuse to associate with.
59. Oxymoron—a figure of speech where two contradictory terms appear in conjunction—giant shrimp, military intelligence, Texas University.
60. Paean—a song of praise or triumph.
61. Palpitation—throbbing or trembling; what old ladies in the South get.
62. Perdition—damnation.
63. *Pyrrhic* victory—a battle won at such great costs that even the victor is a loser.
64. Queue—a line of people; a pigtail. I love how this word is spelled.
65. Quisling—a collaborator; fifth columnist.
66. Rapacious—grasping, predatory.
67. Redact—edit for publication; revise.

68. *Retsina*—a wine flavored with resin. The stuff I drink when we run out of everything else.
69. Rhinoplasty—nose bob by a plastic surgeon.
70. Rowel—that thingamajig at the end of a spur.
71. Ruminant—an animal that chews its cud. If you think this is where ruminate comes from, you're right.
72. Rusticate—retire and live in the country. It doesn't mean get rusty; then again, maybe it does.
73. Saccharin—sugary, sentimental, overly polite.
74. Salubrious—healthy, pleasant, agreeable, Old Bob-like.
75. Scabrous—rough, indecent, salacious.
76. Sententious—fond of pompous moralizing; affected. See how many adjectives there are for Arthur?
77. Sisyphean—endless and fruitless; like Sisyphus, whose job in Hell was to push a stone uphill that immediately rolled down again. See Hogan, Robert.
78. Sobriquet—nickname.
79. Solipsistic—the view that you are the most important, perhaps only known thing in the universe; self-centered.
80. Somnambulant—a sleepwalker. There is a fine opera called "La Sonnambula." Guess what it's about.
81. Specious—superficially plausible, but actually wrong.
82. Stanchion—a post or pillar; an upright support.
83. Succubus—a female demon; sexual predator. Neither of my wives fully qualified.
84. *Tabula rasa*—clean slate; most often used to mean naïve, or never having thought about something.
85. Taxonomy—the science of classification.
86. Thrall—a slave of a person or power or thought. Used with the word "in." It's actually kissing cousins to "enthrall," which means to captivate, but in a good way.
87. Tractable—easily handled; docile (people); pliant, malleable (stuff).
88. Travois—two joined poles pulled by a horse to haul heavy things like teepees.
89. Tumultuous—noisy; agitated; uproarious. Hard sumbitch to spell.
90. Ululate—howl or wail. Some Indian women do this, and it's scary.
91. Unctuous—unpleasantly flattering; oily. Close to obsequious.
92. Ursine—like a bear.
93. Vagary—whim or caprice; most often used as "vagaries of fortune."

94. Vernal—pertaining to spring (e.g. vernal equinox).
95. *Vox populi*—public opinion; general verdict. Run kicking and screaming from this.
96. Wainscot—wooden paneling on the lower part of an interior wall, usually the dining room.
97. Whelp—young dog; puppy; brattish child.
98. Wizened—shriveled-up.
99. Xenophobia—deep dislike of foreigners.
100. Zenith—the highest point; a time of great prosperity. Opposite of nadir.

Study hard, Jackson. I'm counting on you.

Sex, drugs, revolution and the dawn of the Peace Corps. In 1963 volunteer Jack Harjo sits in the jungles of Costa Rica pondering three questions: is there a greater good; does it apply here; and can you really trademark Panama Red, Acapulco Gold and Maui Wowie?

ABOUT THE AUTHOR

Jack Shakely is the award-winning author of "The Confederate War Bonnet," and "POWs at Chigger Lake." His collection of short stories, "Pretty Boy Floyd's Clarinet and Other Tales of Oklahoma," will be published in 2014.

In previous incarnations he was president of the California Community Foundation in Los Angeles, a newspaper reporter in Oklahoma, a US Army officer and a Peace Corps volunteer in Costa Rica.

He is a native Oklahoman now residing in California.

CPSIA information can be obtained at www.ICGtesting.com
Printed in the USA
LVOW06s1549010514

384060LV00003B/619/P